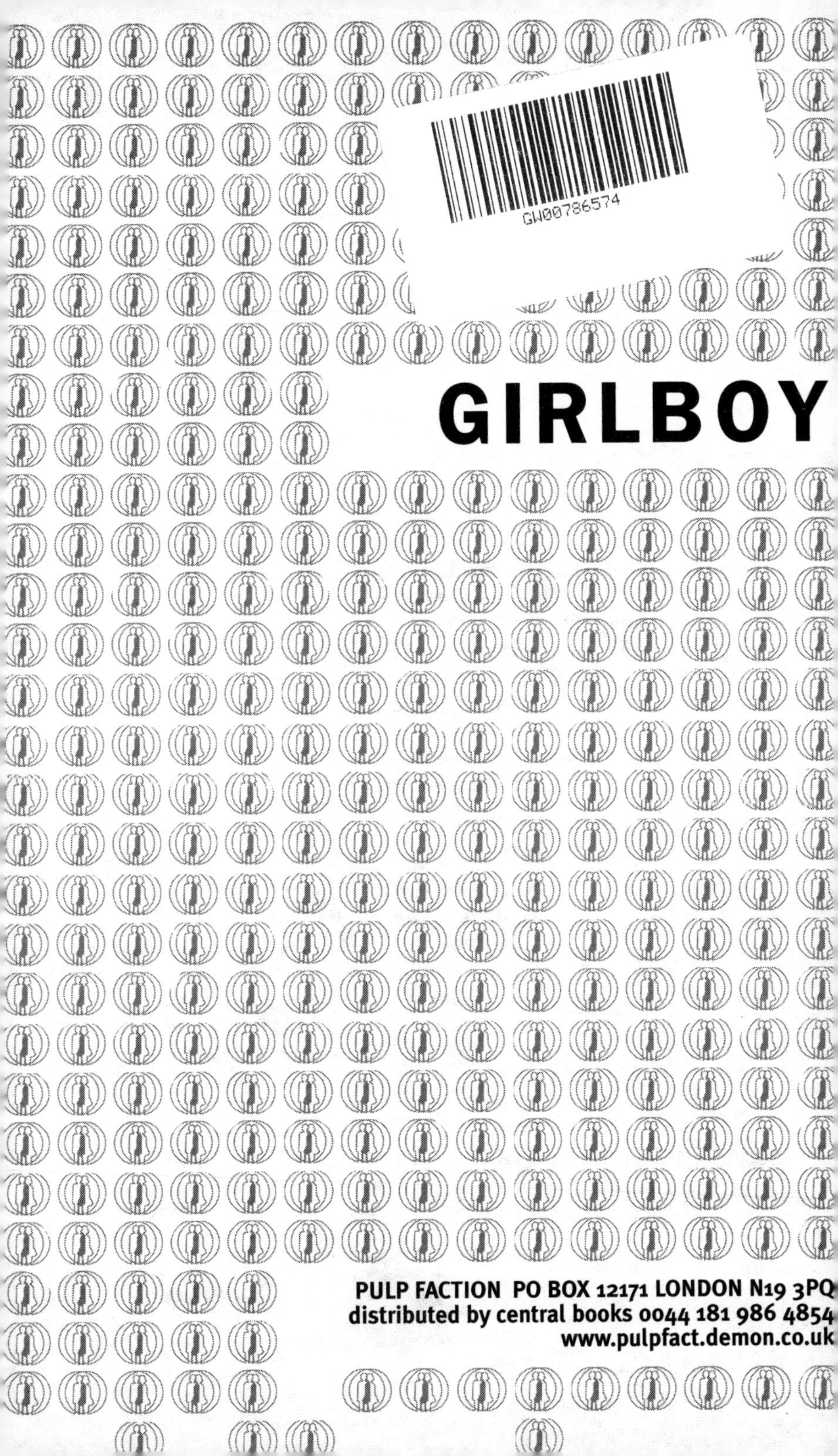
GW00786574
GIRLBOY
PULP FACTION PO BOX 12171 LONDON N19 3PQ
distributed by central books 0044 181 986 4854
www.pulpfact.demon.co.uk

First published 9.9.1999 by Pulp Faction

Printed by Cox & Wyman Ltd.,Reading.
ISBN: 1899571078

Editor Elaine Palmer
Cover design BigCorporateDIsco
Inside pages design Kim Gehrig & Kojo Essuman
Distributed by Central Books 0181 986 4854
Website www.pulpfact.demon.co.uk
Thanks to The Arts Council of England, London Arts Board, John H, Fran and Stevie, Juliet M, Alex at the PO Box, Waterstones Charing Cross Rd, all the writers and artists who sent their work in, and everyone who's bought a copy.

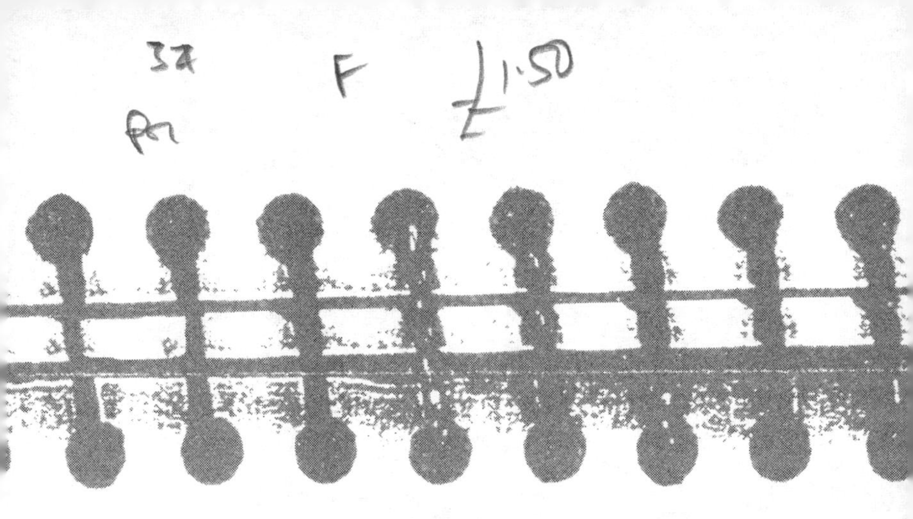

contents

Lipsore 4 Laura Pachkowski
Alphabed 9 Toby Litt
A Lemming Named Desire 20 Richard Guest
Circles 27 Daphne Glazer
Stubble 36 Salena Saliva
Across the Courtyard 38 Matt Thorne
Decor 45 Steve Bishop
Just Juice 54 C Byrnes
A Night of Three Halves 61 Bunny
The Promise 71 Morrigan
Post-Human 86 Anna Landucci
Jump 88 Sparky
Split 90 Nik Houghton
No Time for Icecream 100 Ian Cusack
Ladyboys of Koh Samui 105 Bee
Puppy Fat 113 Martin Sketchley
Hitch Hiker 124 Salena Saliva
Author Notes 126

RIGHT, SO WHERE WAS I?

YEAH, MY NEXT BOYFRIEND WAS A SPECIAL FX MAKE-UP ARTIST.

HE MADE MONSTERS AND CORPSES AND CRAP LIKE THAT FOR HORROR FILMS.

I was at this party and there's this guy and he's bitching about how his agent rips him off and how, like, none of his work survives the director's cut and how he has to decorate his flat with exploding heads 'cause there's nowhere else to put them, and they're works of art and I'm thinking good for you. I hate agents. I'm talking estate, recruitment, literary. All of 'em. Secret agent. Agent Orange. Agents armed with smarmy desperation. Doom. Death. I'm talking Mexican Day of the Dead here. They're all the same.

Anyways, I'm like, nodding and stuffing my gob with guacamole and this guy stops, mid-stream monologue, walks over, pushes my bangs aside and says, 'Smashing widow's peak!' and as I'm choking on this tortilla he asks me what I do for a living and I say, 'Secretary in the city but I hate it, got my RSA after 2 years on the dole and a bust for Possession,' and throw in Class A, in case he's thinking I'm some sort of hippy chick chopping hash in a teepee in Hackney somewhere, and he's like, impressed and stuff and we go back to his 'cause the party kind of sucks and I feel old and craggy with all these retro-hippy chicks in utilitarian mini skirts and hot pants pattering around.

Normally, I hate white guys.

THEY'RE ALL THE SAME. BUT THIS JULIAN GUY LIKED THE SHAPE OF MY SKULL, WHICH IS A LITTLE KINKY, AND KIND OF COOL, SO WHY NOT?

We get to talking and he's showing me these prosthetic scars and wounds and silicon, black-eye pieces that are totally realistic and I get this idea and ask him if he can make me a pair of prosthetic boobs, big wobbly ones, you know, to glue on and rip off? Julian sort of examines my chest and says, 'Why, of course' and I'm thinking of the commercial possibilities of this while he hits the dimmer switch on his human pelvic bone lamp and I get to thinking why, if he's so shit hot at like, reproducing reality, why doesn't he make himself a prosthetic penis but as I'm rolling out of his bed a couple hours later,

I'M FEELING ALL WOOZY AND SOFT AND GET TO THINKING THAT MAYBE THIS COULD BE THE START OF SOMETHING REAL FOR A CHANGE.

So like, a month later, we're eating at this snazzy Mexican joint in Hampstead and he's staring at my face and I'm like, Oh my God, he's in love with me, just what I need right now and he drags deeply on his ultra low tar cigarette and says, 'Darling, I have to tell you, your foundation is completely wrong for your skin tone.' I'm like, gobsmacked and thinking Christ! Two hours in front of a cracked mirror and I'm grossing him out! So, I'm like, marching back to the Clinique counter at Harvey Nichols, real swish, with these pale dead women with stretchy faces and I demand a full refund because they sold me TawnyBrown when I know damn well I'm Ivory and this superbitch says, 'Madam, you can only exchange your goods. It is not our policy to give cash refunds...but may I interest you in Tawny Ivory?'

I hate make-up women. Cosmetic Agents. They're all the same.

Then I find myself working flat out, doing butt-busting overtime as a secretary for 3 generations of toff at Mssrs. Harrow Harrow & Harrow on Cannon Street to make enough dough to get a proper make-over and buy some decent clothes 'cause Julian's allergic to my mohair jumpers and I had to pay Julian's rent too, 'cause he's freelance you know and there was a lull in the British Film Industry, and everything. But I guess I wasn't busting enough butt because I fell behind with my own rent and got evicted from my bedsit in Islington but who the hell cares anyway?

Problem was, I started to miss Julian. He wasn't too thrilled about having to visit me at the hostel—**FOR SOME CRAZY REASON THE OTHER RESIDENTS USED TO THROW SAUSAGES AT HIM.**

So one night I packed my stuff, 3 banana boxes and 2 garbage bags worth, and got a mini-cab over to Julian's gaff in Camden and he's like, fairly cool about me moving in and as I'm unpacking, I'm thinking WOW, this really could be the start of something wonderful and then he tells me not to wait up for him 'cause he'll be pulling an all-nighter in Kensington. He has to do a plaster body cast of that actress Della Devine who wants her body immortalised in bronze which is fair enough I suppose but then I get to thinking about him smearing polyurethane alginate and crystacal plaster all over her boobs and in between her legs and I start to feel a little funny, but I don't wanna get jealous or envious or green or anything like that and anyway I gotta keep up appearances because Julian's working and he needs to concentrate when he's working so I say 'Great! Where'd ya get the job?'

And he says, 'My agent.'

THAT'S WHEN THINGS GOT REALLY WEIRD.

Toby Litt

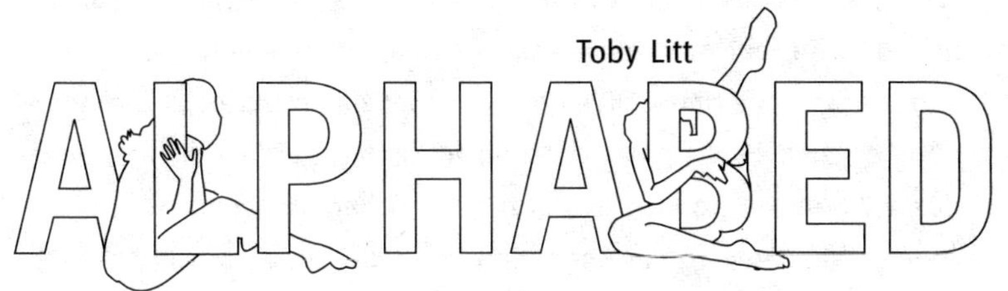

(Sections to be read in any order
other than the one printed)

R. An impulse to fuck her from a new position comes over him. But he can't think of one they haven't tried. He turns himself round so his head is near her feet. 'What?' she says. 'Yeah,' he says. Somehow she understands. That was how it worked, these days. She turns so her back is facing him. Now, this was going to be tricky. He wants to slide it in, but everything is at a strange cutting-your-hair-in-the-mirror angle. His penis slides between her damp buttocks but not into her cunt. Her feet are close up to his face, dirty soles. He doesn't want her to kick him in the face when she comes. If she comes. When she comes she tends to thrash about. No, it isn't working. He turns himself round again and lies back.

C. There is something comforting to her in the squalor that surrounds them: the damp sheets, the dirty room. It confirms to her that she is bad. Her forefinger strays down his side, bumping over his ribs. Abstractedly, she brings her forefinger up to her eyes and examines it, as if expecting to find

a scurf-crescent of dust upon it—as if, she thinks, she were her own mother coming into this room and interrogating the mantelpiece. Slattern, that's what her mother would call her. Slatternly, that's what she is. A brief glow of the old disobedience flares up in her lower spine. If what she is doing here is something her mother would disapprove of, then it has to have some virtue. This thought makes her for a moment almost happy.

N. He turns her over onto her front. She resists, a little but not much. He forces her legs a little apart, so he can kneel in-between them. Again, she resists. 'Hey,' he says, and she relaxes. He is between her legs, now, looking up the bed towards the pink velour headboard. Her back is a totally present slab of flesh. At times like this, he is capable of losing all interest in her. He forces his knees further apart, forcing her legs further apart. 'What?' she says. For a while, he waits—doing nothing. Then he strokes her cunt gently, upwards, once. She moans, from pleasure or impatience. He lies down at her side again.

J. The pleasure they used to give each other—as she remembers it—sometimes lasted hour upon hour. Now, it has become something begun out of brief desire and ended, as soon as possible, in deep disgust. Once, she would lie back as he constructed another language of praise, vowel by vowel, consonant by consonant, upon the unparallel lines of her cunt. Once, he could see his way through to new worlds of allure, following the hints of her flicking tongue. Now, it is all aboard for the smalltown mystery tour they have already twenty times taken. Now, their bodies are familiar laboratories in which nothing more original is bred than contempt. Once, each touch was pure exploration and improvisation. Now, preprogrammed subroutine, Basic or C++. These contrasts make her wrinkle her eyelids up in a slow-motion flinch. He notices but doesn't say anything—certainly not what he has been thinking.

O. He gets up to go for a piss. When he gets into the toilet, he has to wait a while for his erection to go down. He tries thinking about unsexy things: carpets, old men, warts, surgery. None of them seem to work. In fact, he is surprised to discover, the thought of surgery makes him harder than usual. She would be waiting for him, lying there. 'Fuck,' he whispers. He braces his hands against the toilet's narrow walls. This is not good. He looks down and notices his penis has become flaccid. The thought of her must have done it. This is even worse. He pisses for what seems like a very long time. It is more satisfying than his last orgasm. He drips himself off and walks back through into the bedroom without washing his hands. As he is lying down, his skin touching hers again, his erection comes back.

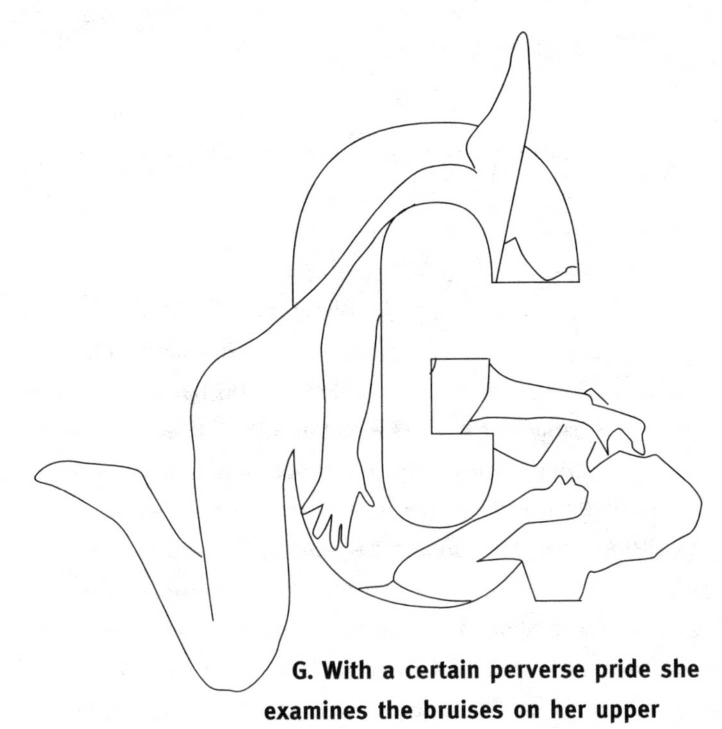

G. With a certain perverse pride she examines the bruises on her upper arms: blue, brown, yellow, green. All the dull and bright colours flesh employs to express its belated resentment. This is where he holds her when he holds her down. It is a weird kind of consent that she gives to this force—at the time, she resists it; before, she forbids it; after, she complains about it; but overall she recognises that it is necessary. Otherwise she might smash a fist into her own mouth or buck so extravagantly that he would slop out of her. Hard as it is to credit, she does still sometimes completely lose all control. 'Look,' she says, holding her bruised arm up in front of him. 'Look,' he says, and lifts his nail-torn hips up from the bed. She miaows and makes her hand into a claw. He beats his chest and grunts.

W. He likes her neck the most of all of her. With his hand, he makes her tilt her head back so that her neck is elongated. He kisses the place where it dips above her sternum. If that particular kiss in that particular place weren't one of their worst sex-clichés—like her running her fingers through his hair and jerking his head back, like him thrusting three fingers inside her just as he was about to make her come with his tongue—the action would almost be tender. He kisses the curve upwards to her chin, but stops short of her mouth. She strains to lift herself off the pillow, to reach upwards, to give in to his tease. But he isn't teasing. He really doesn't want to kiss her on the mouth. She falls back and so does he.

L. She gets up to go to the toilet. He languidly tries to grip her ankle, to hold her back, to make her beg for the privilege of leaving his company. She jerks her leg away, hard enough to convey hatred. There is an argument here to be had. If he wants it, she will give it to him. He falls back on the bed with a thump that is louder than it need be. This annoys her even more, but she continues out of the bedroom—nude and barefoot—into the toilet. As she pees she feels a strange gathering-up inside her, like the slow roar of a kettle boiling. She looks down into the

toilet bowl, expecting to see streaks of bloody gunk. Nothing. She smells her fingers. She can't remember when her period is due. The roar in her abdomen subsides to a hiss then crackles out. My funny body, she thinks. She isn't able to come up with anything more adequate. Her mind isn't working like it used to. She stands up to wipe herself. As she drops the paper into the bowl, she tries to sense what he is doing in the other room. Walking back into the bedroom, she regrets not having stayed away longer—not having taken the opportunity to steal a little more respite.

U. As she is now lying with her eyes closed he is able, for a while, to watch her. He doesn't think she is asleep. More likely, he suspects, she is trying to get his attention by playing dead. Sometimes, when they were in bed like this, she would play to his worst fears and deliberately stop breathing. By now, he's become accustomed to this trick. But, to start off with, he wasn't able to tell exactly what was wrong. He would just become incredibly anxious and believe that his own death was imminent. Then she would start breathing again, as quietly as she could. His anxiety would lessen, but not disappear. Then, one day, he caught her at it and started beating on her chest. She exploded into laughter. If she tries that trick on now, he decides, he will hurt her more than usual when they next fuck.

B. For no reason that she is consciously aware of, she begins to cry. There are whole areas of remorse within herself that she doesn't have the capacity to deal with. Not at the moment. Not at this exact moment. She senses—as she has sensed them before—darkness and density. There is a screech, not sound, but halfway between white noise and feedback. Instinctively, she turns away from it—swerving into an obvious action: grabbing hold of his penis and dropping her head down onto it. The taste in her mouth—of him and her and her and him, intermingling, seemingly forever—the taste disgusts her into thinking about how little she wants to be doing this. Any of this. So she stops. 'Hey,' he says, a very long way from understanding what's just happened. Miles and miles.

Z. He reaches down with his thumb and inserts it part way into his foreskin. The sliminess that he encounters is nothing more than he expects. This is the state that they themselves are tending towards: deliquescence. A few more days of this, he thinks, and they will flow off either edge of the bed; they will seep into and through the colourless carpet; they will stain the floorboards and wet the wiring; they will drip from the nicotine-brown ceiling of their downstairs neighbours' flat; they will obey gravity all the way down into the ground. He pulls his thumb out and draws a slime-line heart on the nearest of her buttocks. This is one of their previous languages. But, this time, she is unable to decipher the sign. 'Again,' she says. He pretends to repeat the action, drawing a question mark instead of a heart. 'Okay,' she says, and lies back with her arms held over her head.

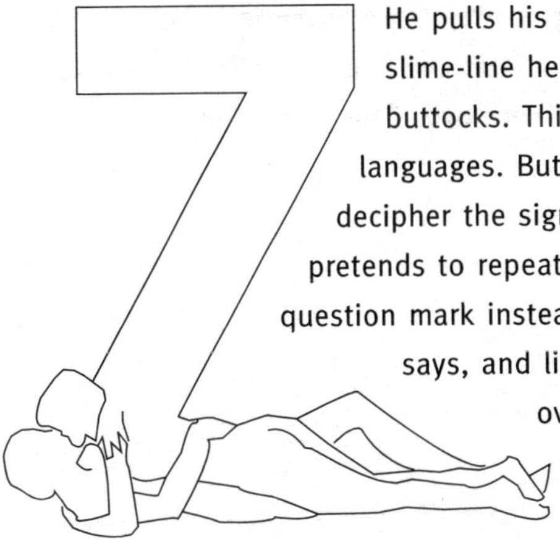

M. Death is something she tries not to think about. She pulls the sheets up over her head, in attempt to dark-out the thought. But the dark—fittingly—only encourages worse images. Dying while fucking. Dying while being fucked. Him dying on top of her. Her going into spasm and him not noticing. Him trying to say something final and her sobbing too loud to hear him. The one left alive—him or her—and all that would happen

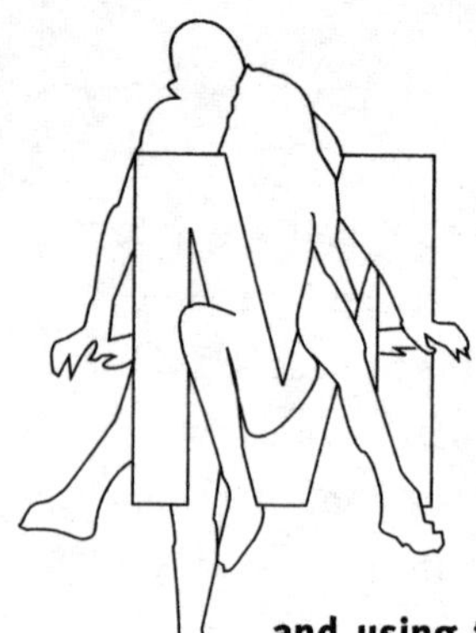

to them. Standing holding the telephone after dialling 999. Men and women entering the flat wearing heavy fluorescent clothing. Professional voices expressing professional concern. A complete stranger making a cup of tea and using the wrong mug. Answering questions there is no point answering. Old women glancing up and down hospital corridors. Emotions starting only at the epiglottis. Vomiting. Retching. Aching to vomit more. Only retching. Crying. Confessing. And at the end of it all, at the very end, the release—like birds flying out of the top of her head. Or his.

V. He is aware that, unlike most people, she is uglier asleep than awake. There is none of the usual relaxation in her face. Her lips continue to pout, like the spout of a small milk jug. Sag-lines dent her cheeks, as if she were a much older woman. In fact, and this is the cruellest thing, he can imagine her five years, ten years older. And she is no longer—in this imagined future—a woman he wants to have anything to do with.
There are rings round her neck: one for both completed decades of her life. This number will increase. Her cheeks will become heavier and even more slablike than they already are. The lines at the corners of her eyes will be there constantly, not just at moments of hysteria (laughter or distress). He is hoping that

she is asleep now, although he can tell that she isn't. He is afraid that somehow she will be able to sense how cruel his thoughts have become. If he were a decent person, he'd get out of this bed. He would speak honestly. One of them would have to leave. But he isn't a decent person. He doesn't get up. Instead, he grips her nipple between his thumb and forefinger. She pretends to just be waking up.

The thirteen other letters of the alphabet are at

www.pulpfact.demon.co.uk/babylondon

PROGRAM FOR THE CREATION OF A SHORT STORY

Paragraph No.	No. of Words	No. of Adjectives	Theme	Time
1	204	12	Intro - Character	now
2	187	11	Girlfriend leaving	then
3	170	10	Retiring (to bed)	now
4	153	9	The ceiling	then
5	136	8	Events of that day	now
6	119	7	Conversations	then
7	102	6	The countryside	now
8	85	5	Jokes	then
9	68	4	Clothes	now
10	51	3	Why she left/Media	then
11	34	2	TV/Food	now
12	17	1	Masturbation	then

* then = 1984
* now = 1996
* I always kill the thing I love
* The only viable form of rebellion is in wasting resources
* I just don't get it

A LEMMING NAMED DESIRE

Richard Guest

In 1984, I didn't kill the things I loved, I simply wore them out. I gorged myself on TV, music, food; anything that came along. Bright, coloured objects; plain, grey, casual clothes; and clinical, electronic music were the axis around which my body revolved, trying to find substitutes for love. Because love was everywhere, but just out of reach; in the records I listened to, on the radio, on TV, in magazines and books...everywhere.

I wanted it, but I just couldn't get love. From the trials I had done on my own I was certain that, with another person involved, its possibilities were inexhaustible. But I didn't socialise (outside college), and thoughts of specific girls, or love in general, always brought with them a whispering, jealous anxiety, for example: Once you've got your girl, what will you do with her? Where will you take her? How will you keep her entertained?

I did not act on love, until September. In the meantime, I paced about my family cell, listening to the same songs over and over again; hearing nothing beyond the stylus crunching into position on the record's edge; the songs merging with my longing and the nights that always accompanied it.

Jules has just left, slamming the front door behind her, perhaps for the last time. It's difficult to tell with her. She wouldn't let me touch her. I sort of understand it, but...

I see her slouch away into abstraction through the door's leaf-patterned glass. When the pink dot of her bare back disappears, I turn and walk into the kitchen. Then I walk out again, and walk into the living-room, sit down on the sofa, stand up, and walk around, looking at nothing in particular. I've seen it all before.

What is it about her? She's blonde, but she has a big nose. Her breasts are firm and inviting, but her buttocks are manly...there's always this tension. And she doesn't understand me, or the conflicts that lie knotted at the root of our relationship. She is not, and never will be, my girlfriend. I thought she understood that. I thought that was what she wanted.

I walk out of the lounge and ascend the stairs. Once inside my bedroom, I turn on the stereo, select a record, plop it on the turntable and take off my shoes.

I must have padded around the room for a while, picking up the rhythm from the record occasionally, tapping it out with my feet and fingers, but without really listening.

I was no longer letting anything in. I hadn't been for quite some time. TV seemed to make no sense, or else was too boring to watch. My mother's cooking was bland; so food was a chore, and I ate it so fast, and in such quantities, that I couldn't taste it anyway. I had no energy for reading and, in any case, always read the same eight books. The only magazines I could manage were soft-porn, which made me fear for my eyesight.

I lay down on the bed; first in a foetal position, then on my back (as if laid out in a coffin). My room, at the time, had walls and furnishings that were royal blue. I did not sleep. I lay there with my eyes open. It was four o'clock in the afternoon and it was raining.

The ceiling is white, and textured with little nipples, and half-formed droplets. I imagine, as I did when I was five, how it would feel beneath my feet; walking around up there, climbing over the wall at the top of the door, and passing lights that now sprouted from the floor. From up there, I could see the house from a new and vertiginous angle; every object a curio, no longer demanding use (like furniture in a doll's-house). Like I was God. Up there, life would be simple. People could be kept at a distance. My family and friends could become my acquaintances.

I roll away from the idea, and face the wall. Nothing there, but a lack of colour and a few fingerprints. I study them. I recognise them as my own. Then I imagine myself, seen from above, rehearsing the moves of a restless sleeper, for nothing.

At 3pm (the end of her college day), Jules came over. We climbed the otherwise empty house, and briskly entered my bedroom. She took the easy-chair, opposite the bed (on which I arranged myself so that I had the best opportunity of seeing up her skirt, nem.con.). For half-an-hour we volleyed sentences back and forth, teasing out innuendo, prodding our words into suggestive shapes. And Jules laughed with great heaves of her chest, rocking in her seat, alternately exposing and cloaking the sweet tunnel between her thighs. My trousers grew tight. A roll-call of well-rehearsed arguments against getting involved with her scrolled up behind my eyes: Our families, our friend's advice, fashion, her nose, the size of my penis, etc.

I couldn't take my eyes off her, but couldn't act, either. Contact was always accident.

We talk about Karen, and the problems she has with her mouth. Jules tells me about the less conventional things Karen has done with it,and how frustrating it must be for her, having it wired up. In breaks in the conversation, I suggest activities to Jules, that might lead to accidental frottage.

Me: Do you want to play a game of something?

Jules: No.

Me: Let's paint each other's feet.

She demurs, obviously preferring the erotic tension in our inactivity. My suggestions become fleeting spurs for conversation. She provokes me with her mouth, eyes, legs, thighs, nose even, but gives me no opportunity to act. Why not?

Me: Do you want to play a game of something?

From the bed, I strolled down the lane to happier times. Two innocent quarries trembled in the bushes, as her serious older brother hunted us; sweating and cursing in the undergrowth.

He was an obstacle. David had the jealousy that apparently mars most brother-sister relationships, and I felt his interrogative gaze on occasions, boring into my face, the back of my head, my hands; anywhere he might find a clue to...

"What are you doing in there?"

"Hiding."

"Well, come out. You're caught now."

Occasionally, he had what seemed like irrational rages, and it would be fair to say he frightened me.

"Tell me a joke."

"You know all my jokes."

"I promise, I'll laugh."

I want to see her laugh, and she knows it. But more than that, I want to touch her. I sit up to show her this. I dig my bare toes into the wool of the carpet. For the first time today, she sees the rigid shape of my penis, through the worn denim of my jeans. She wets her lips, cheeks blazing.

"Go on; joke."

"Ok then, there was this Englishman..."

I'm surprised those grey jeans could take the strain. I wore them day-in, day-out, changing them for another identical pair only when they needed washing. Once I'd decided on this uniform, I no longer wanted to experiment with colour. There must have been something comforting about the convenience of constantly wearing the same clothes. It took me years to realise that my clothes were not attractive to anyone.

So, we get to the end of the joke, (which isn't funny). She rocks back and forth with no real conviction, smiling. Silence.
My erection has started to fade. Disappointment comes on in her eyes like a bathroom light. We silently ponder the end, as seen in swirls of carpet pattern.

I didn't care, when she got up and left (at 4pm on Wednesday August 3rd 1984), because she never acted the way I wanted her to (submissive; stupid); the way women acted on TV.

After much loosening, I grab the problem by the neck,
and wring the life out of it.

Going to see somebody in prison is different from hospital visiting. You can't go walking in with a packet of ciggies or some chocs or a cassette or anything. Plus this woman tells me when we're just about going in, that they might even body search you in case you've got drugs up your you-know or whatever. It's disgusting.

The prison's really like you see on telly and in films. It's a massive old redbrick fortress and there's a perimeter wall and an electrified fence. In front of it lorries are bouncing along the road all the time on their way to the docks and the ferry terminal. As you're going up to the window to say what you've come for, you feel like you're a criminal, the way the uniforms look you over.

There's women with bairns clinging on to them and some bawling their heads off. I wouldn't bring a bairn in here. I've left Mark with Mam. You get to see some proper slags in the visits room and they're showing everything they've got.

This officer gobbles me with his eyes, points me to a table and tells me I've to sit on a particular chair. I'm wondering what our Dave'll look like after all this time. I'm feeling real nervous, what with the slags and the officers staring at me.

Then he comes striding in. Our Dave's real good-looking, except he can't stop blinking his eyes.

'Hiya our lass,' he says, 'how you doin?'

'Or right,' I say, though I'm not really, but you have to say something.

'How's the bairn? You should have brung him in.'

'You're jokin...not in here—anyway, I couldn't have managed the buggy on the bus.'

'How's our Mam—thought as she might have come as well?'

'She's busy with her new toyboy, Ryan—he's a proper know-it-all. What's it like here then?'

There's this prison officer earwigging like mad, so I talk real low.

'S'or right—they can beat your friggin' brains out for your trainers though if you don't watch it. I've handed mine in.'

'Oh...'

I can't stop looking round. I bet loads of these fellers are murderers and rapists. When I was little, whenever the bus went past the nick, I'd be staring out at it. It kind of scared me to death but I wanted to see inside. Our Dave's eighteen now, two years older than me. All the time I've been expecting, he's been on remand in here—seems like forever. I'm not real sure what he done—well, he says he never...

'So what's new?' He's blinking real fast but smiling.

'Well, me and Andy are getting wed—it's going to be next month like—a white wedding, all the trimmings, you know. Perhaps you'll be on the out by then, do you think?'

'Yer, yer,' he says, 'bound to be,' and he smiles, a real dizzy smile.

He's gone thinner and I notice he's got all these marks on his arms, like scratches.

'What's them?' I ask. He gives another swimmy smile.

He isn't going to tell me. It's secret.

'So what you been doin' then, Dave?'

'Nowt,' he says, 'they're all crack-heads in here.'

'Is that right?' I say.

There doesn't seem to be much to talk about.

'I'll get off more than likely.'

'Yes,' I say, 'then you can come to the wedding.'

'You bet.'

'There's quite a few lasses I know, who'd like to go with lads in here—they've been asking me to get 'em pen friends.'

'No problem,' he gives his funny laugh and his eyes twitch. 'As a matter of fact I could do with a bird myself.'

'I bet you'd like Joanne, she's a mate of mine, was expecting when I was.'

'What's she like?'

I have to describe Joanne, and we talk a bit more and then it's time to go.

'I'll be at that wedding, our lass, you just wait.'

I feel real sad when I get out in the road and kind of uneasy, like after I'd first gone with Andy and I knew something wasn't right—I felt different—of course, I'd fell with Mark but I wasn't to know it until I had that pregnancy test from the chemist's. Mam just said—'You stupid little bitch, you should know different.'

Anyway, that's all water under the bridge. In two months time I'll be Mrs Appleton and that'll be that.

Seeing Dave like that has unsettled me. I'm getting this disgusting gone-off smell like bad drains in my nostrils. You can just about taste it. I've been having a dream as well, where I'm locked in a toilet and can't get out. I keep banging on the door but it's one of them real old toilets with thick dividing walls that go right up to the ceiling, and nobody hears me.

With me being in a state of nerves I ask Joanne to look after Mark for me while I go off on my own. I've said I'll have her Sammy tomorrow so's she can go and see Dave in the nick.

I get the bus off the estate early on. There's all these fellers in the suits even though it's real hot. It must be court day. If it hadn't been, they'd still be in bed.

The grass is the colour of a smoker's fingers and it's nearly dried up in Queen's Gardens and there's white fluff and pigeon and duck droppings all over. A load of winos are sitting on some benches in a corner and they bellow at me: 'Come on sweetheart, let's gie you one!'

Some lads are playing football. They'll be students from the college behind the Wilberforce statue. There's lasses draped on the grass under the trees, snogging lads. You can see their belly buttons where their tops are riding up, and the lads are letting their hands go all over. Some have their eyes shut and they're panting.

It's that hot I can feel myself running in sweat and I start wondering what I've come here for—it'd be better to go and have a look in the shops, but then I see this kid staring at me. He's real tanned and his white blond hair is cut in a number two so it looks like stubble. His eyes are as blue as the sky, no kidding—because I look up and I can't see a single cloud and then I look back at him. I've sat down on a seat in this little garden. Opposite me a couple are snogging each other and some old bags are pulling faces.

'Hiya,' he says, 'can I sit here?'

'Suit yourself,' I say.

'Want an ice, then?'

'Yer,' I say, 'go on then, or right.'

So we wander across to this cruddy place and he buys me a cone.

'What's a lovely girl like you doin' in here on your own?' he says.

The black bits in the middle of his eyes are growing big. He's licking his cone and I get to see the pink insides of his mouth. His lips are quite thick. I start wondering what it'd be like to be kissed by him. I mean, there'd be this soft cushiony feel—it wouldn't be like have a plassy band rubbed across your mouth, would it? They'd be soft, they'd suck you and you'd be on fire. His aftershave's real spicy. It makes me think I'm in that Indian shop in town.

'Are you one of these dumb blondes then?'

'Mind who you're calling dumb blonde,' I say.

'Oh, it's like that is it!'

He's joking, perhaps he thinks I'm just a little kid. I get a shock sometimes when I wake up in the middle of the night because Mark's bawlin' and I think—ehup, he's my bairn, I'm a Mam... I've always wanted to be grown-up but now I suddenly wish I was just me like I was before I had the bairn.

'It's not like anything,' I say, thinking I'd best be moving on. I'll just finish the ice and then I'll say tarra.

'Come on, you never answered my question.'

'Just came for a walk, anything wrong with that? Anyway, what about you? Why aren't you at work?'

'Merchant Navy...just home for a bit.'

'Do you like it in the navy then?' I've always wanted to go on a ship, go somewhere else real different...see something a bit unusual.

'It's or right,' he says. He tells me about some of these countries he's been to. It's like magic. I've not been anywhere, seen anything, except once to Costa del Sol with Mam and one of her boyfriends when I was little, but that didn't seem much different from Blackpool from what I remember.

'Want to come for a drive?' he says.

We find his car on the multistore. He drives real fast and I can't stop looking at the golden hairs on his arms.

The town goes flashing by, all these streets with rows of houses where people do the same things day in day out. I can just imagine the women, changing their bairns and putting nappies to soak in the buckets and sterilizing feeding bottles and vacuuming and doing the windows—lists of things every day and you can't stop doing them.

When we're driving, this scaredness comes on me, because every day in the paper you hear about lasses getting raped and murdered and everything. All I know about him is that he's called Shane, and he's real good looking and kind of easy with it.

Down by the estuary it's real quiet. The water's the colour of grey satin and it's bumping and jumping on the black pebbles. It's not the summer holidays yet, so all the kids'll be in school, sitting at their desks and the doleys won't be out of bed until later. Andy'll be in his boiler suit under some car at work. Joanne says I'm lucky he's marrying me.

We get out of the car and climb a low wall and walk down to the water's edge.

'Do you always bring girls up here?' I say.

'What would I do that for?'

His aftershave smells real strong and hot in the sun. I look at his skin and it's golden brown.

We start walking along by the water and there's pieces of wood that have been washed up and green weed with shiny navy-blue flies dodging over it and everything smells like the swimming baths, mixed with tar. We can see the Humber Bridge from here and the cars shooting across it look like dinkie toys.

'It's great that i'n it?' Shane says.

'Yer,' I nod my head, though really it makes me go all cold and clammy because of what our Dave told me about this kid who was padded up with him, jumping off of the bridge when he got on the out... Only it didn't kill him...I can just see him flying through the air like a closed umbrella, falling and then going splat—he didn't burst open like a tomato hitting tarmac though, he just drifted out to sea.

We carry on walking and he holds my hand. After a while we come to a grassy bit that's edging the sand and the pebbles, beyond that there's a railway track and the rails are gleaming like knives. He pulls me down on the grass and we roll about and he kisses me and it's how I thought—these big plushy lips press on mine and his tongue's in my mouth and it's slippery but then firms up and works over the roof of my mouth. It's like he's trying to explore every crevice of me. When he takes off his 501s and his polo shirt, I see he's tanned all over and there's not a hair on him: he's beautiful. I've never seen anybody as beautiful as this and that's the truth.

He unbuttons my top and I slide out of my trousers and we're lying there doing things when there's a great roar and the ground shivers and an Intercity goes ripping by and folk are staring out of the window at us and I can feel myself going red. They'll think I'm some slag—a slapper who'll go with anybody. But it's not like that. We have a good laugh and we lie in the grass for a bit, sunning. I don't tell him about the bairn and that I'm getting married or anything.

After that I see him nearly every day because I bribe Joanne by saying I'll mind her bairn a real lot. I've told her I'm ill really and I have to go to hospital for tests.

We do it everywhere, even on top of a multistorey carpark. I don't care if people think I'm a slag.

On the day he goes back to sea, I'm with him in a taxi going down to the dock. We pass the nick where our Dave's locked up and it seems real weird that I just can't walk in there and say hello. Shane asks me if I'll write to him and I say yes, but I know I can't. We're both crying when he walks away and I'm still crying all the way back into town along that bumpy grey road with the dust swirling.

Everybody says I look real young and beautiful at the wedding. Dave doesn't get out for it. He's at court the same day. In the evening we have a reception at this club my Mam knows on our estate. The DJ's got everybody up bopping when I see our Dave's friend, Wayne, coming in. He makes for me. All of a sudden I feel real shivery.

'Hiya, Wayne,' I say, 'what you drinkin'?'

'Don't mind me,' he says, 'I just came to tell you about your Dave in case you never heard.'

'Oh yes,' I say.

The DJ puts on an Oasis track. I'm trying to concentrate on Wayne but I'm a bit drunk and I've got a sinking feeling in my chest.

'Your Dave's been sent down for life.'

'What!' I say. It's boiling hot in the room and I feel dizzy.

'Well, they said—"at her majesty's pleasure"—and that means, he dun't know when he'll get out.'

'But he said he never done it.'

Wayne shrugs. I'm thinking about this great white ship with the black and white striped funnel, sailing on sea like glass and the sun's blazing and it's all real peaceful. They're steering towards an island and there's palm trees and white beaches and green and red parrots flying...

coming soon
from pulp
faction...
edited by Patsy
Antoine, a
collection of new
stories from
Courttia Newland,
Joanna Traynor
and others
AFROBEAT
NEW BLACK BRITISH FICTION

I WISH I HAD
STUBBLE TODAY.
MY GOD,
I WISH I HAD
STUBBLE TODAY.

STUBBLE

SALENA SALIVA

NOW, IF I HAD
STUBBLE TODAY,
I WOULD WEAR A
VEST COVERED IN
STAINS AND GREY,
I WOULD HAVE PISS
PATCHES IN MY
TROUSER CROTCH,
I'D HAVE HARD ROUGH
HANDS TO TOUCH.

I would make a bet or two on a horse,
Spend all the rent on whiskey, of course,
Then I'd slap my woman if the mashed potatoes got cold,
Then I'd yell at my sons to do as they are told.

Then I would shag the barman's wife,
And get barred from that pub for the rest of my life,
I would piss through the letterboxes of anyone who ever pissed me off,
Put my sweaty balls in the hands of a nurse and cough.

**IF I HAD STUBBLE TODAY.
MY GOD, I WISH I HAD
STUBBLE TODAY.**

I would flash my hairy dick in an old rain coat,
Make a pearl necklace around a young slender throat,
Then I would drink with the most magnificent thirst,
Then lazy sweat fuck until I came first.

Although I may not have stubble on my face today,
I lost on the horses, my vest stinks and it's grey,
I've drank a shit load of beer and there is whiskey on the way,
And I've beaten my lovers to let me have my own way.

**FOR WHO NEEDS STUBBLE
TO BE A CUNT.**

Matt Thorne

across the

When my mother went into hospital to have my sister, she gave me a toy elephant. Inside the elephant was a tape-recorder, and every time I squeezed its stomach, the elephant spoke with my mother's voice. For the time she was away, I began to think my mother had turned into the elephant, and I was very surprised when she returned with a baby girl.

Looking after two children proved more irritating than one, and my mother soon decided to return to work, taking a job at the nearby Community Centre. The Centre was split into two separate buildings, one for men, the other for women ***(although this being the tail-end of the seventies, there was a unisex toilet).*** Both buildings were frequented by young, unemployed men and women from the surrounding area. Most of the women were mothers and brought their babies with them. My mother worked in

courtyard

the women's building, and consequently I spent much of my time there. The women who came to the Centre were hungry for attention, and I soon discovered that I was going to see a lot less of my mother than I had before.

Before long, my mother had her hands full, and I was entrusted to the care of a girl called Joanna. Joanna was nineteen years old. She was doing a photography course at a nearby technical college and was helping out at the Centre during her Summer holiday. I fell in love with her immediately, finding her a much better substitute than my elephant, especially as she at least spoke with her own voice.

My memory of Joanna is unsurprisingly sketchy. Although mum has many photographs from this period, it seems my friend was camera-shy. The only record I have of our relationship is a handful

of crayon drawings which ***(if they are to be trusted)*** suggest she had blonde hair, a purple head, a green body and blue arms and legs. She also had a dazzling smile and no neck.

I spent my time with Joanna constructing childish narratives which she would explore with me, becoming any character I requested. We spent our mornings drawing and making up plays, and our afternoons acting them out. There was no audience for our performances and we would frequently stray a long way from the Centre, reimagining the surrounding urban sprawl as we expanded our ideas. Tensions often ran high while we were away, and we'd frequently return to find women in tears, and broken chairs.

For those two months, Joanna acted as my guide through a world I didn't really understand. Most of the women who worked in the Centre were committed feminists, and although they didn't tend to discuss their beliefs while I was around, I could sense new complexities being introduced into my existence. Many of these were light-hearted ***(I remember a long conversation about the logic behind 'man-sized' tissues and whether the implication was that men had bigger noses)***, others clearly required more thought. There was also the physical reality of group child-rearing going on around me, and although I quickly became blase, I remember an initial anxiety at seeing nappies getting changed and babies being breastfed.

Most of the women had partners who went to the men's building across the courtyard. Although sometimes the two groups would mix in the lunch-hour, their morning and afternoon breaks were staggered to reduce the danger of confrontations. One of the things I enjoyed doing most with Joanna was sitting with her in a window-seat and sometimes we would watch the men as they prowled around the courtyard drinking plastic cups of coffee. Often she would offer to take me down to talk to them, but I felt too shy, wanting to keep Joanna to myself.

Every now and again, Joanna would be unable to come in and I'd have to spend the afternoon either sitting in with one of my mother's groups or waiting in the office alone. When I was in the office, the other women who worked in the women's building would come in and check on me. I looked forward to their interruptions, and would waylay them with stupid questions. Although they were prepared to indulge me, I could sense their irritation at being away from the action and got used to answering their questions by nodding and saying 'no, I'm fine.'

My mother's employment at the Community Centre coincided with the start of a trial separation from my father. They had never been a particularly happy couple, and babies and foreign holidays had failed to cement their bond. They had decided to settle in the town where my father was born, and my mother missed her family. Money had been tight, and for the last year they'd been forced to move in with my grandfather, who was not the easiest of men. My grandmother had died young, and ever since then he'd drunk heavily, often returning from the pub to lecture my parents about their failures.

Most of the other people working in the Community Centre had reached similarly pivotal moments in their own lives and there was a sense that everyone was attempting a new beginning and conversations tended to focus on the future instead of the past. The only time anyone talked about their families was when they were describing the frustrations involved in maintaining relationships with their parents.

The only frustrations I felt during this time were directed towards my father. I loved going through flash-cards with my mum and learning to read and write, but I refused to take any interest in the things my father tried to teach me. I wouldn't allow him to show me how to swim, ride a bike or play guitar. I supposed I considered these masculine activities, and wanted nothing to do with being a man.

I don't remember talking about this stuff with Joanna, although it must have influenced my imagination at the time.

Some time later I got sent home from infant school for trying to strangle a girl. Apparently, we'd spent all afternoon hiding in the trees kissing, and then something had gone wrong. None of the teachers knew what to do with me, especially as before then I'd showed no signs of violence, and was incredibly repentant after I'd been caught.

Joanna left at the end of the Summer. I kept drawing and writing, but didn't show the results to anyone, hoping that this was some sort of test and if I could prove myself she would come back to me. Surprised by the depth of my misery, my mother decided I needed a change. So she asked one of her male friends in the building across the courtyard if he would mind looking after me for an afternoon.

I remember this man taking me over to the other building. Not wanting to be difficult, I ignored my anxieties and followed him inside. The first thing I noticed was the difference in the decoration. The women had done little to alter their space, and aside from a few knick-knacks, hadn't marked out their territory. The men, however, had transformed their rooms into a lightless den, tacking blankets over the windows and painting the walls scarlet and black. Several of the walls had cartoons taped across them, and examining the marker-pen doodles I realised there was something here I could borrow for my own drawings.

My mother's friend introduced me to the others. Several of the men shook my hand, and I discovered I liked this formality, feeling

very grown-up. As well as chairs, the main social area had three green bean-bags and I curled up in one of them while the friend found me something to read from the upstairs library. I hadn't really done much reading since I came to the Centre and I was intrigued by the look of the spy story he brought down for me.

Settling into the beanbag, I wondered if I could get used to being in this building and considered whether I ought to feel more comfortable here than with the women across the courtyard. Of course, nothing could compare with Joanna's company, but now that she was gone the women's building didn't seem quite as exciting. I decided to stay on this side for the rest of the day and see how I felt at the end of the afternoon.

I really got into my spy story, although my childish mind was puzzled by some of the odd sadism. The villain had been shot in the testicles by the hero several years before the start of the story, and the narrative built up to a climax where he extracted revenge in a particularly grisly way.

Reading lacked the excitement of my games with Joanna, but at the same time it seemed an adult substitute, and a good way of entertaining myself without disturbing the others. Between sessions, some of the men would start conversations with me, asking what was so interesting about my book. I found it easy to talk to them, and over the next few days began to miss Joanna less and less.

On my last day at the Community Centre, the men and women were going on a joint trip to the local swimming baths. I threw a fit, not wanting to do this activity that reminded me of my father. My mum was especially keen to go on this outing, and she rode over my hysterics, forcing me to come along.

When we arrived at the pool, my mother asked her friend to take me into the changing-room. We went in there together, and I realised with horror that we were going to have to undress together. As he pulled the belt out from his jeans, he said to me,

"So, how come you hate swimming so much?"

"I just do."

"But you can swim, right?"

"No."

"Would you like me to teach you?"

I looked at him. "I don't know. My dad tried...I'm just not very good at it."

"How do you feel about your dad then?"

"I hate him."

The friend was naked now. "How would you like it if I was your Dad for a while?"

I looked at him. "Oh. I'm sorry, I didn't know..."

"What?"

"You and Mum."

It was a question. He nodded, and I felt sick.

Soon afterwards, I started going to school. There were problems, although the strangling incident was as bad as things got. My mother broke up with her boyfriend and started looking for a new job. My teacher replaced Joanna in my affections, and I frequently got in trouble for demanding too much attention from her.

I'm not sure what effect, if any, all this has had on me. I know I look for lovers who will be able to flesh out my fantasies, and I still use books as a substitute. I no longer feel so desperate to be different from my father, and no longer see my mother as beyond reproach. The Community Centre is now a senior citizens home, and although there is still a courtyard, the buildings are no longer divided by gender. I still can't swim or play guitar, although I've learnt how to ride a bike. At least that seems like progress.

DECOR

STEVE BISHOP

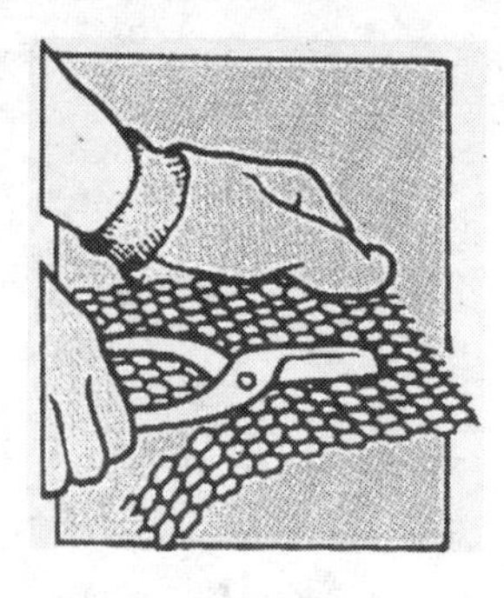

The feng-shui was wrong somehow.

A 60s coffee table blocked the space. The corner of the fake leather sofa was there too much in the middle of the room. And the comfy chair didn't smell exactly but there was ash ingrained in the fabric, so its multicoloured pattern appeared grey, like train seats. The energy between them was all wrong, but there was no other way to arrange the furniture in their little flat.

The dope and ashtray stank was gone, but the murk remained. Opening the window, she heard a noise down the street like a motorbike but it was up in the trees by the park. There was a guy with a chainsaw sitting in the branches. He seemed to finish what he was doing for a moment and left the saw chugging away while he shouted down to his mate. She looked at the little scrap of tinfoil in her hands and wondered if she should.

Yesterday's battle was still fresh on her knuckles. She looked at the grazes and felt a chill. It was the first serious row they'd had since she caught him in bed with the PR assistant from the record company (that's what he said she was—a fucking groupie more like). It's not like he was famous or anything, but well, she probably wouldn't have given him a second look either if he wasn't in a band.

She rubbed her face where he had slapped her. She hadn't really been hurt exactly and she'd laughed at his expression as he'd crumpled to the floor, clutching his swelling gonads and threatening legal action for loss of earnings. Now she felt like having it just to piss him off: but what kind of rationale was that

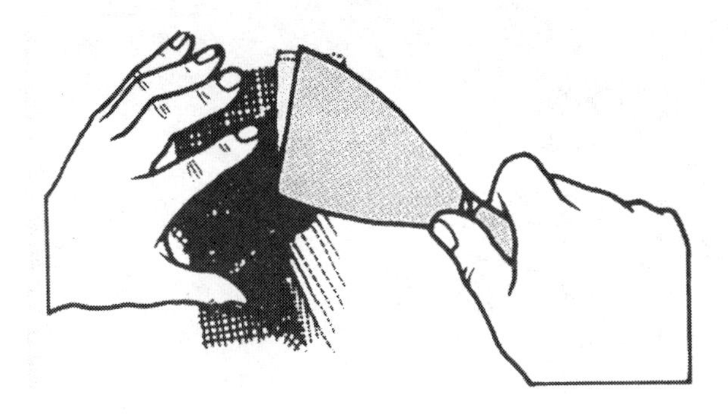

for bringing life into the world?

She was seized by another spasm of nausea and rushed to the bathroom. Diced-carrot cornflakes sprayed against the back of the bowl. The best to you each morning, she thought, trying to see the funny side. Mum always said if you can laugh at your problems, they don't seem as bad.

Back on the yucky sofa she wanted to cry but couldn't summon the energy. How the fuck had this happened? She tried to tell herself that she would really be saving it from the agony of life, but she knew she was just being selfish. What a great birthday this was going to be. Spunky and Rocko gambolled about on TV. Rocko's Modern Life. Even cartoon characters are endearing losers now. There was a card from Mum and an HMV record token for ten quid. Also a letter from the council. The tree outside was ill. They were chopping pieces out of it to make it better.

Retail therapy time. She put a wrap into the pocket of her retro-look leather jacket. It was the unwanted trophy of their first physical fight. Looking at it again, she felt disgusted and empowered at the same time.

She stood and waited twenty minutes for the number 50 bus from Moseley into the city centre. Kids were smoking skunk on the back seat. It made her want to go back home and have a spliff, but he might be back there by now, probably still nursing his bruised bollocks.

She got off by the rag markets, full of amazing, cheap retro

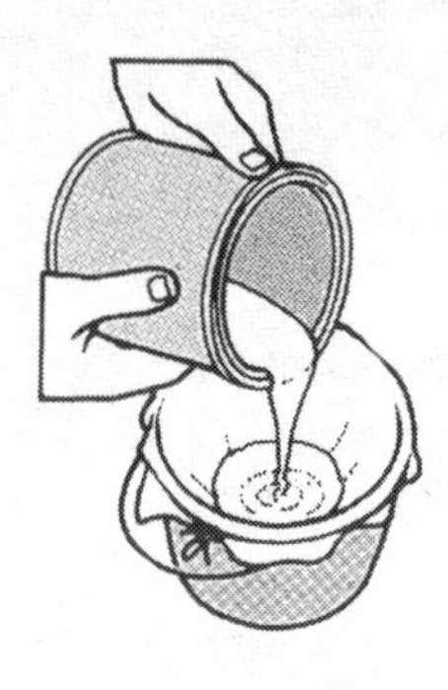

clothes. Stuff that you never saw anybody wear except in student bars and trendy pubs in Moseley: 70s flares, leather jackets with super-wide lapels, cords, ultra-thin rollneck sweaters . And all the other stuff as well. Guys selling plastic shoes, Asian fabrics in fantastically bright colours, pink and green and turquoise with gold sequins and piping, some with little mirrors all over them, crappy electrical goods that would probably break before the batteries ran out, food mixers with butter-knife blades, stuff for making curtains, bed linen, pillows, quilts, military surplus, combat trousers, gas masks, BB guns and bomber jackets.

About twenty women crowded around a big stall where two athletic looking middle aged women were selling jewellery. It was good stuff, fine gold chains, chunky bracelets, real gold, realistic looking diamonds. They were modelling their own merchandise, draped in chains and bracelets. She tried on a couple of bracelets and thought about the ring she'd bought him for his birthday. It was gold with a Topaz in it.

She wandered around a bit more, past racks of sportswear run up in sweatshops on the low rent outskirts of the city, made to look like the real thing but with that extra or missing telltale stripe. The same cuts as the High Street but cheaper materials, without that all important little motif or tag. She realised she was looking without really seeing, things just went through her. She went up the hill to the main market area, past some mad old bloke doing Karaoke and a bunch of dangerous looking Christians with their leaflets.

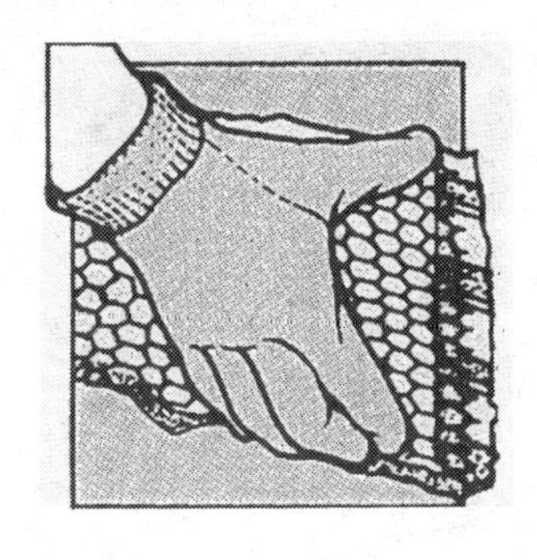

Up the ramp she caught a blast from the chippie and felt sick again. There were more shops in the underpass. More cheap clothes and imitation makes. Up the steps to the High Street and across the bus lane into a modern arcade where chrome, neon and carpet interiors insulted her intelligence. The shopping centre was crowded, it was raining, people smelt. Kids in shellsuits stole and ran up the escalators the wrong way, chased by security guards .

She sat in a sort-of Italian café by the HMV shop, stirring cappuccino and feeling like she was in a video. It dawned on her that she really wanted to get rid of the baby and that there was no way that she could take the experience of childbirth. She felt sicker than ever, but forced the coffee down, needing the energy.

The music store was more chrome and neon. She was tired of her usual dance stuff, there wasn't anything much good new out. He always bought drum and bass, and guitar stuff, she liked club classics and 70s. He listened to a lot of punk. He looked like a film star, the band were tipped to become quite successful. She wondered about getting rid of him.

Looking over at a display of new CDs, she saw the biggest eyes ever.

They had been digitally increased with PhotoShop or something. She bought the CD without even knowing what kind of music it was and left the arcade.

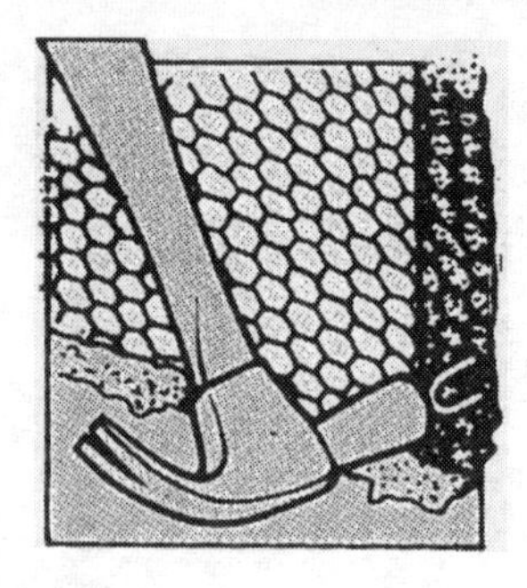

The Brookes advisory well-woman clinic was behind Toys-R-Us. It seemed like someone was having a laugh. Maybe the town planner was some kind of deranged puritan. The law courts were nearby.

She waited about an hour in the medical miasma. There were other girls waiting to be seen as well as her. Nobody said anything much, but one girl was reading a book about witchcraft. She wondered about the strange posters on the walls that warned of obscure medical conditions. Who designed them? Who read them? Were there really people suffering from TB in this city?

The doctor was professionally sympathetic. One of the old school. He had greasy grey hair impeccably combed and raked back over his head with brylcreem.

He told her not to worry; this operation was virtually guaranteed to be error free. Modern technology was very reliable. She would only be in overnight and there was really no need for this simple scientific process to be any worry to her. There was counselling available afterwards if she felt she needed it. She went home, opened up the new CD and remembered the shop assistant's smile as she paid for it. There was a special message in it just for her:

One day the world will be ready for you and wonder how they didn't see.

She cried for a million reasons all at once.

Over the next few days, everything stayed as fucked as it had been the day she found out. He was still in a foul mood. They barely spoke. She wanted to be rid of him too, but what then? His bony body seemed just as fused with hers as the little mushroom-

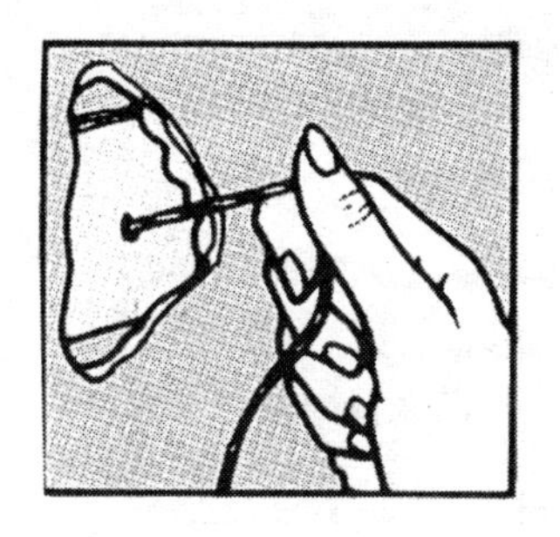

shaped clump of cells that was her baby, growing inside her, soon not to be.

On the morning she was due to go in she was puking again. It wasn't even morning sickness anymore. Outside it was brilliant sunshine. She hated that. She tried listening to her new CD, but the music just washed over her. Good things couldn't touch her today. There was nothing on TV and for once it mattered. She thought about him, taking it all for granted, about the thing in her stomach that wouldn't be there soon, resenting it and hating herself for resenting it, then resenting him again and distracting herself by wondering if it was his and being disappointed to realise it couldn't be anyone else's and then hating herself for that too. She wondered who knew and imagined her friends laughing at her for being a stupid cow and remembering how unconcerned she herself had been when it had happened to people she knew. Life was just normal for other people. She was stuck with this downward spiral of misery.

It was like that Simpsons episode where Marge gets done for shoplifting. Bart wanted Flintstones chewable morphine. All these heads were swimming around her. It was kind of like that only less funny. The chewable morphine gag gave her an idea, or at least something to gravitate towards. She put her hand into the pocket of the retro-look leather. The little wrap of foil was still there from their fight last week. She smoked it off a scrap of bacofoil and crashed out on the floor.

She was lucky to get to the hospital on time, sleeping much

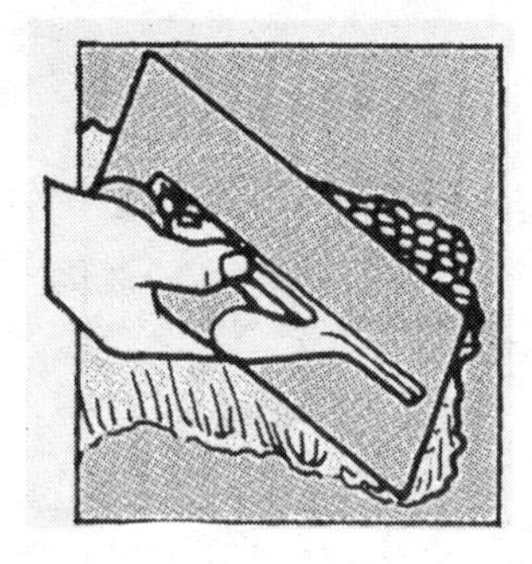

longer than she wanted. The bus was a nightmare. She had to stand but her legs kept buckling under her. Eventually an old man stood up for her. The old dears around her said things like It's the heat, I expect before trying to pass on sage old lady-type advice.

It was a desperate day at the hospital too. The staff were jaded and overworked. In another ward on the same day a woman lost all her sextuplets.

A tired and harassed nurse showed her to her bed without even bothering to be polite. A plastic mask was put over her face. The anaesthetist gave her more gas and she went out again.

She got back still woozy from the drugs. He hadn't been around for a while. This was definitely the end.

She found herself thinking about feng-shui again. The baby's body was gone. The spirit that lived inside it had gone back to live with the other spirits. The furniture was too frumpy. The chair had wooden handles on it. She hated wooden handles. The coffee table was too low and too obviously 1960s, not sick enough for kitsch, not stylish enough to be a classic, just shit.

Outside she could hear a chainsaw. Chips of fresh wood were spewing out of the tree. She wandered downstairs to the street, not really knowing why.

She sat and listened to the buzzing of the saw for a while and then the guy stopped for a break. He came down out of his tree. He was a demented looking skinhead with tats.

She gave him her best smile and said:

—Could I borrow that thing for a while?

The 60s table was first to go. Flying smithereens of formica danced onto the two quid rag rugs. Next the fake leather sofa. It died with a horrible rending shudder as the blades ripped through the plastic and hit foam and wood. A chipboard cupboard set fell like a card house and disintegrated with the lightest of touches from the chainsaw, the rickety chairs, desk and lamp soon followed. Finally, she cut up the comfy chair.

Half an hour later they sat giggling in the room filled with impossibly broken chunks of wood, foam, plastic and ripped up fabric.

—Top buzz, eh? said the skinhead. I bet you're flying inside.

And she was.

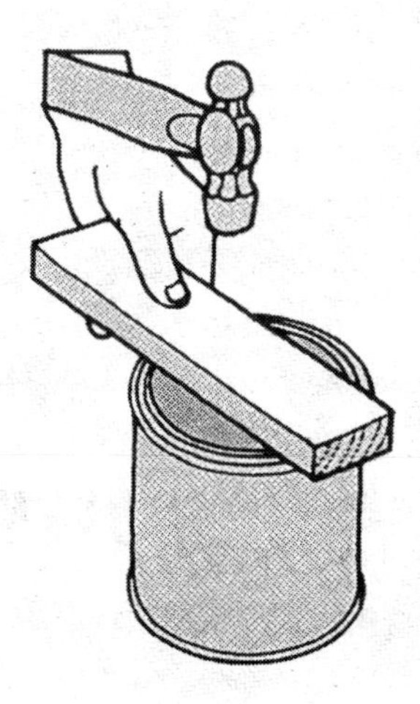

C BYRNES

CELIA IS SITTING IN MY KITCHEN CRYING. I OFFER HER ANOTHER CIGARETTE, TAKE ONE MYSELF AND (IN A NOW UNCONSCIOUS ACTION) FLICK THE ZIPPO INTO LIFE WITH ONE HAND. MY LEGACY FROM COLLEGE: AT LEAST IT TAUGHT ME SOMETHING I SUPPOSE.

As I bring the cigarette to my lips I smell Nathan on my fingers. A morning of chain-smoking has done little to eradicate his scent. A mixture of aftershave and the polleny, rich, heavy smell of males on heat. 'Love Juice' the glossy magazines call it. Ridiculous. There wasn't any love in the drunken advances of abusive fathers, nor in the amorous fumblings of spotty youths. Just juice, desperate spawnings. The smell does not repel me. Somewhere a long way off, Celia is crying again.

'HOW COULD YOU DO THIS TO ME? I THOUGHT WE WERE FRIENDS.'

The ash trembles at the end of her flailing hands. It's going to fall on my floor, I can tell. I push the ashtray towards her in the hope that she will notice.

'I TRUSTED YOU.'

Her voice, I notice with mild interest, has the same desperate pitch as my mother's. This is what real middle aged women sound like. I am living a lie and yet I'm happy.

'I am your friend Celia.'

If I continue to smoke at this rate I shall be sick. Vomiting itself does not bother me but I hate that feeling when you've smoked too much. The slushy greenness in your chest; the swimming, pressured sloppiness internal organs take on when they react to poison overload. Give me a whisky headache every time.

Now the thought has occurred to me, I fancy some. It helps to trick the body out of rejection, you can smoke more and pay for it less. I don't bother asking Celia whether she wants a whisky or not, I know she'll drink it.

'I am your friend.'

'THEN WHY,' SHE PLEADS, 'DID YOU SEDUCE JOHN? HE'S MY HUSBAND!'

I roll the question around in my head. There is actually very little point in all of this. Celia will think what she likes and nothing I can do or say will make any difference. It couldn't be his fault, of course not; that leaves me or her. If I can prove it wasn't my fault then she will have no choice but to bring all that guilt and anger down on herself. Poor Celia.

I'm trying to concentrate. Slowly, irresistibly, Nathan's image comes creeping into my mind. Gradually I remember the sensation of putting my finger into his mouth and probing the softness of his tongue. The recollection makes my heart race. I put my finger in my own mouth. It feels similar, setting off the same sexual response. I feel my stomach tighten, a warm tingling stabs at the lower part of my body and begins to spread towards my hips. The aching makes me want him desperately, right now. If he were here I would take him on the table top and Celia could find her own way out.

Celia reads my silence as guilt, she is crying again and beating herself with an invisible stick. I feel nothing for her. Why shouldn't I tell her what she wants to know? Why shouldn't I tell her that John had come round drunk, that he had cried like a baby about his terrible life and loveless marriage. How he confessed that he'd always wanted me, lay awake at nights thinking of me, masturbated over me whenever Celia gave him the space and privacy to do so.

If we were better friends, we could laugh together about his pathetic attempts to kiss my mouth, his tongue lolling and hands grasping and moving incessantly. I could tell her how he looked like he was having a fit, how I was tempted at one point to call the paramedics. It wasn't worth thinking about let alone having a crisis over. She should kick him out. Join the growing ranks of women like me who feel strong and beautiful.

I met Nathan at the seafront. I was surprised when he told me he was sixteen, I had thought he was older but I knew he couldn't be much above twenty-one. I've learnt to recognise them, the college boys, heads full of chewing-gum and cheerleaders. You're shocked now, I can tell. Don't be so conservative. I've been sleeping with eighteen year olds since I was thirteen, I have a taste for them. I didn't suddenly wake up one morning fancying teenagers, I just never grew out of them. There's always some pretence of a relationship of course, although you both know its hopeless. One, maybe two, weeks of blissful fucking and then it's over. I've never approved of one night stands.

Nathan was different. All night we had lain together in each other's arms, exploring each other's bodies with an innocence I had long ago forgotten. We did not kiss, we did not make love, we didn't even 'talk', just gently groped at each other through the darkness. It wasn't that he was beautiful, he wasn't: but he had an attraction that stunned me. He had charisma. From behind thick glasses his long-lashed eyes expressed a tenderness that must have been a result of projection on my part and myopia on his.

God knows what actually went through his mind, probably nothing at all but I had the sensation, for the first time, that somebody thought I was really beautiful. Not just a sexual beauty, an inner beauty. I felt loved.

I didn't like it.

I'm sure if I had confessed my sins or told him something of myself, he would have bolted. Yet, lying in the dark, I had the impression that I could tell him anything and he would not turn away. His skin was warm and I thrilled to the touch of his fingertips as they brushed my hair, my arms, my lips. I wanted to kiss him with every molecule in my body but knew that I could not break the spell that we had tacitly agreed between us.

I will not see him again, although I want to. I will not see him again because I want to. I can't afford to have my calm routine uprooted. Tonight I will put on my short dress and go to the seafront again. I will find some boy and screw him until Nathan drops out of my mind. If I can't find anyone suitable, then I will phone John. I'll tell him how Celia came round here giving me a hard time and demand that he take me out to make it up to me. I couldn't sleep with him of course, not because of Celia but because I don't fancy him. He'll do for an escort though, his attentions should drive Nathan out of my mind long enough for me to get drunk. In a day or two I will have regained my calm. I just need to buy a little time.

Celia's face is red and swollen from the disgusting fuss that she's been making. It seems astounding to me that she can care that much. Don't get me wrong, I'm not a callous bitch or anything, there are lots of things that deeply move me but the fictitious transgressions of a long-time married man are not among them. Celia is still smoking, the pile of ash at her feet has been increasing throughout the morning. Again I roll the question of guilt around my head.

'Nothing happened you know.'

As soon as I've said it I feel the futility of this line of reasoning. She will not be pacified.

'THAT'S NOT TRUE,' SHE'S SCREAMING NOW, 'JUST BECAUSE YOU DIDN'T FUCK HIM DOESN'T MEAN THAT NOTHING HAPPENED. YOU BETRAYED ME. YOU PLOTTED BEHIND MY BACK TO STEAL MY HUSBAND.'

I'm tempted to tell her I wouldn't touch him with a barge pole but I can't. I can't rattle her existence with such profanities.

'I was jealous Celia, jealous of your life, your home and your kids.'

It's what she wants to hear. She stops crying at last. She takes my hand in hers and I can smell the whisky and stale cigarettes on her breath.

'I KNOW,' SHE MUMBLES, TRYING TO COMFORT ME 'I'M VERY LUCKY. I UNDERSTAND HOW LONELY YOU MUST GET SOMETIMES. I'M HERE FOR YOU. WE'RE FRIENDS AREN'T WE?'

Her sense of superiority has returned and there is a look of calm satisfaction on her face. I can tell she feels safe again. Safe that her miserable existence is worth something, safe that she has something that someone else might want, safe that her life is not yet over.

I need to get out of this kitchen. The evening is a hazy, brilliant, August one. I can see a seagull circling above my tiny patch of back yard. Above the smoke I can smell the tide going out, and Nathan. I must shower. Down at the seafront the bronzed and empty-headed Adonises will be cruising.

a night of three halves

Bunny

The train plunges into a tunnel and at once becomes three—one real and two illusory. Everyone looks at themselves looking back into the carriage. David looks up instinctively. He thinks he looks alright tonight. The collar of his coat is wide and it flips up at the back. His hair is long on one side at the front. He sucks his fingers and pushes the spit curl behind his ear. He rearranges his long legs under the table.

The train seems to keep stopping every three hundred yards and when he finally gets into Birmingham, David is singing: 'Are you sure you wanna be with me? I've nothing to give.' Too loud, probably.

Outside the train station David meets Mikey, the object of a hundred nights of fantasy fucking. He is shorter than David remembers, but that is probably because they'd been sitting or lying down for most of the time of their first meeting. He is definitely fatter. David can see already, even through the bulk of his clothing, that Mikey is definitely fatter. But he doesn't mind that, doesn't mind that at all really. Fat is good he thinks. He likes to have something he can push himself on to, push himself into. When David first met Mikey he was thickwaisted.

'Now he's fat,' he thinks.

When David first met Mikey, it was the end of the summer. David had been working for this film production company. Just out of college, glowing with knowledge, but desperate to shed his shiny skin. He started smoking and got a tattoo: three cherubs and a swirl of red fabric floating just above his left buttock. One cherub (the one with the slightly evil face) was playing a lute, another the flute, and the one inbetween had his arms stretched wide, his eyes heavenwards—and his mouth open.

It seemed to David that he'd done things a little bit the wrong way round, but he'd been a considerate student. David was one of the few people who felt privileged to study what he was studying, where he was studying. So he made the effort. While other people were tripping through lectures, dropping E's and subsidiary subjects, David was necking his boyfriend and only dropping his trousers occasionally.

So there he was, now dying to be part of the adult world, still wet behind the ears and the ink on his arse not yet dry. So he worked for expenses and was grateful for the experience.

On the way back home to Manchester after a hard day's shooting, David got stuck in Birmingham. There was a train strike, and all the coaches were full and it just didn't look hopeful. He didn't know what to do, so he wandered around until he found this likely looking bar. He went in, and there he met Mikey. And Mikey's boyfriend—Paul.

There was David, skinny Jewish boy, stretching and yawning, about as bored as a bored boy could boring well be sitting boringly. He just wanted to be at home—to crawl into bed and sleep the sleep of someone who had been standing around in a film set since six a.m. making tea and having the piss taken.

David could see him staring, but he ignored Mikey. Mikey bad blood shot eyes and soft, nicotine yellowed hair. Mikey Woolworth's trainers and yellow fingers. Most importantly, Mikey hair out of the top of his shirt. Thick, soft, white, manhair. Maybe he wasn't ignoring Mikey, maybe he was looking back. David. Mikey.

David took the last cigarette out of the box out of his bag, stuck it in his mouth and chucked the bag on to his shoulder.

'Have you got a light please?'

'Course,' said Mikey.

(Always works—why everybody smokes).

'Haven't seen you before.' Mikey held up a light, 'Visiting?'

'Yeah,' inhaling, 'I'm waiting for my coach connection.'

'Oh,' said Mikey, looking at the boy with the long fringe, which was still in tatters after an encounter with some Domestos. Bad hair was okay, it showed that you cared about looking like you didn't.

'I'm Mikey and this is Paul.'

Later on, they were all three naked and David was feeling like an over inflated sleep over mattress about to explode with the excitement of the weight of two men.

'Come 'ere,' Mikey had said and they had kissed and Paul had undressed them quickly while they kissed and kissed. David struggled to hang on to his pants, wanting to feel cotton on cotton, their stiffness bumping, sliding inside, over one another. But the only thing that stayed on for a single minute were his socks. So moulded to his feet were his handknitted socks that Paul was wrestling with David's ankles to take them off and nearly knocking David off his feet in the process.

'They are good those socks that yer Grandma knits fer yer, aren't they?' he said. Paul's voice reminded David of a local radio presenter on one of those programmes where they asked things like 'Why does yer skin go wrinkly in the bath, eh? I just don't know, why does that happen? If yer know the answer, give us a ring and yer can have a mug.' David didn't know whether disliking that kind of chat made him a snob, or whether it made him a discerning listener or if maybe the two things were the same anyway.

So David crouched down to yank off his socks and Paul was there, swallowing the whole of his cock, just taking it silently. And Mikey's was right there in front of him, so David just pulled it in his fist and put it into his mouth.

'You wanted us from the moment you saw us, didn't you Dave?' said Mikey, slit eyed in ecstasy.

'Mmmm,' said David, partly because his mouth was full and partly because he didn't like talking at this moment usually. Which was tough because Mikey really got off on it.

'I'm gonna make you scream, tonight boy,' he said 'I'm gonna fuck your hole.' Hips gyrating, nice and slow. 'You'd like that wouldn't you?'

'Er...' David had said he didn't want penetrative sex, but it didn't stop Mikey going on about it like a child about chocolate on Easter morning. Somewhat misplaced, thought David, and downright dangerous as well. Something about ruptured bladders and comas.

Anyway, it wasn't until later that David realised that was just how Mikey got off, talking like a porn film and everything. Even after he realised that Mikey's sexual banter was nothing more than fantasy, David found it a bit hard to get along with. Mikey didn't compliment David while they were making it, he just talked about himself—sort of. The words 'Yeah, SUCK that DICK' were to be planted in David's head that night and stay there forever like an evil totem exchanged in teens.

At the end of this, David decided that Mikey was the one he really fancied, but Paul was the one he really liked. And this was the way it stayed this second time he met with them. This deliberate time.

It was only this second time that it occurred to David as to why Paul had such a lovely hairy chest and belly, but his back and arse were clean and smooth. He shaved it. This, of course, disgusted David, whose penchant was for the mature, hairy and unslender man.

But then the thought occurred to him that maybe Paul didn't shave himself but that Mikey did it for him. Mikey did it so that he could feel him clean and smooth when he fucked him. And David imagined them standing in the bath, Paul very still while Mikey drew the razor through the soap on his back. There was no soundtrack to this short film, no grunting and shouting fantasies of obscenities. But there was the drip of the tap into the inch of tepid water in the bottom of the tub, echoing in their tiny bathroom. Then the soft scrape of metal across skin and the plop as Mikey shook the foam and tiny black hairs spattering across the tiles and into the bath. Just the sound of two people doing something carefully and intimately together.

Would you like to shave me Mikey?

Back at the pub, where they are drinking the second and final time they meet, David sits alone twizzling his half of Guinness on the wet bar, waiting for Mikey to come back from the phone where he's been talking to Paul.

He comes swinging back, big grin on his face, big beer gut.

'He's had a sleep,' he says climbing on to the stool 'One minute he was watching Neighbours on the box, the next thing the phone rang. Hurhurhur.' Mikey looks right into David's face and they think about later.

At the bar is this boy with the blackest hennaed hair and a fringe that has been cut with a ruler. He takes a small rectangular mirror out of his pocket and smoothes his flat front flap of hair with spit moistened fingers. David can't believe that flap head thinks his cut is so cool he has to keep checking it out. David thinks he looks like Jim Carrey in Dumb and Dumber. Dummy. David tries not to look at him because he can see he's looking back. The dummy says: 'It's haircut day today,' and David thinks he is referring to his spit curl and feels uncomfortable. But then David realises that the dummy is talking about himself and someone else.

Me, yes, I've had my hair cut today too—can you tell?

Standing at the urinal, David gobs a Guinness-coloured glob which slides down the white porcelain like gravy. He pisses it away and is spelling D-A-V-I-D-A-N-D- and then his piss drops off. He doesn't wash his hands.

When he gets back to the bar, Paul is there.

'Hello!'

Paul is no different than before. Except maybe his hair is longer. David prefers short hair.

'David, how are you?'

'Excellent thank you, what are you drinking?'

'Oh no, David, let me take you to this new pub, you'll love it there it's just around the corner. C'mon.'

David stands and is putting his coat on. Paul is standing already.

Mikey says he thinks he'll just stay here and David goes off to see the new bar with Paul. It seems strange to David, first being only with Mikey and now just Paul. He wonders if they're playing some sort of game with him.

David does not want to be alone with Paul. They will not stay long at the new bar, just another swift half. Someone near the door jiggles unselfconsciously to techno.

'I think this back room is really great, y'know with the plants painted on the ceiling,' David interrupts Paul who is telling him about his holiday to a hot island where 'sex is very available, do you follow?' And about this boy he knows who's 'gorgeous and rent, but gorgeous do you follow?'

'I said, I think it's really clever—these plants painted on the walls and over on up the ceilings.'

David is glad now they are back with Mikey and he finishes his final half.

'Let's go now I'm tired.' It's David. He means it, he is tired, it's been a long day and he works hard but he's been thinking about David and Mikey and Paul every minute.

But Paul's got the day off tomorrow and so he wants to make the most of it, 'do you follow?' So he's going to hang around a bit longer, but he'll be home soon.

Mikey is dropping Paul off at some pub close to their flat. He is parking the car. David and Mikey are waiting for the lift. An alsation called Lottery nudges the back of David's leg while they wait, causing him to start. It looks at him with dopey eyes, takes a ruffle on the head like a poisoned biscuit and ambles off again. The lift pings, the doors slide open with a sound like David's Father sharpening the knife to cut the roast and David cringes and Mikey taps his foot with his finger on the dooropen button.

'C'mon David lad,' he says.

The lift is a sickening ride, then they are inside. Inside the flat. Inside Mikey and Paul's. The city has dropped away below.

They are alone, David and Mikey, and after he puts the kettle on for some tea they are on top of each other almost right away. David can hardly come up for air, Mikey is so keen. Later, David will miss those kisses that suffocate him so, when he has a lover that doesn't like to kiss.

David is a bit worried, he is wondering, what will Paul think? Or does he not fancy it with him tonight? He knows that Mikey is the one he fancies but he wanted Paul to be there too. He wants to be kissed and to be sucked at the same time—that is why he is there again, after so many months.

Or what if Paul is on the pull? What if he is going to come home with another young man and expect David to be enthusiastic about that? What?

David manages to get Mikey to the living room, slips off his trainers and sips his tea but they are soon kissing again, one eye on the rugby on the telly, one eye on each other's pants. David continues the pretence that he enjoys the rugby so the telly stays on. Mikey goes into David's trousers, so David pops open Mikey's jeans. The fly slides open with the push of breathing fat belly and white hair all over, and his cock just bounces out because he has no pants on and that disgusts and disappoints David at the same time.

By the time Paul rolls in, David and Mikey are rolling around on the sofa, naked. Happy boybody and manbody, bumping and bouncing and feeling and scraping.

'Hi,' says Paul, hanging up his denim jacket and glancing at them casually as though they are playing Scrabble. He's alone David sees. Paul goes into the kitchen.There is a sliding window in the wall, so you can see neck to belly button of whoever is in there. David watches Paul making a cup of tea. Mikey and Paul have all the Tetley Tea Folk—small plastic characters from a tea commercial, collected with tokens from petrol stations. The fact that Mikey and Paul have the whole set seems to highlight their suburban meticulousness.

'I'm having some tea. Either of you guys want some?'

Mikey comes up for air. 'No thanks Paul, I'm having a beer'.

David is finding this all a little bit strange. But he's happy.

Paul comes in blowing across his tea and slurping it gently. It is an Ed the Duck mug. Mikey will tell David for the second time, the second morning, as he drinks out of that same mug:

'You think of an idea like that Dave, and it takes off, it'll make yer that will, it'll make yer yer fortune.'

All three of them sitting up in the bed will contemplate this in silence for at least a minute.

Paul's clothes are off and he clamps himself on to David's dick. He stays there for the next twenty minutes. David has to push him away from time to time to stop himself from coming.

'Shall we go into the bedroom?' says David for the third time. His bottom is sore from all that scraping on the carpet and the old sofa which now seemed unbearably bobbly.

All three rise. Three naked men. Paul isn't stiff. David doesn't really realise yet that Paul is an arse man and thinks Paul's lack of erection means lack of arousal.

Paul goes to the armchair, where a pile of cuddly toys sit orderly under a small blanket with chewed up corners. He selects an old panda, squashed flat from nights under his weight and faded from window sill summers and washing machine winters. Smooth across the back and droopy at the front, Paul lifts the panda up to his face and inhales, turning slowly from side to side.

'Each one of my friends has a story David,' he says, without a trace of irony. 'Each one has a special memory, d'y'follow?'

David hates the panda. He can't bear to see Paul with this stuffed toy. It makes him feel sad and guilty doing what he is doing. David just wants his kicks, he's bored of being nice. His tattoo is ruling, the cherubs are dancing on his backside tonight.

'Let's go to bed.'

They're in the bedroom. David is kissing Mikey and squeezing his soft white hairy breasts. Paul is standing by the dresser, opening a condom which he puts over Mikey's cock which somehow seems smaller to David, now that it's dressed. Still kissing still squeezing still pushing. Paul is standing, stooping slightly and lubing his backside. Something about the way he is standing reminds David of Nice N' Sleazy by The Stranglers.

This second time, away from the initial, restrained masturbation session they had last time, David realises what Mikey and Paul really like. That Mikey wants to fuck and Paul wants to be fucked. MikeyandPaul.

And so that's what they do. It might be safe but in David's eyes it's not kind. MikeyandPaul writhes around a bit, while rubbing smooth back with open hands and eyes closed imagining it's MikeyandDaveyandPaul, and managing to get a mouth over David's cock at the same time and shouting, 'Oh! What am I doing David? What am I doing? Am I fucking you?' and David is watching MikeyandPaul and he is coming. MikeyandPaul comes but David's not really sure if it's just Mikey now.

When Paul slides off Mikey, Mikey's yellow johnny has the little sad pouch at the end but David can see that the yellow purse is full of dark liquid and he can't help but look there and he wonders if it's blood or because Mikey smokes and he can't help but look.

During the night, David wakes up with Paul's mouth over his cock and he can see him looking up like a golden retriever bringing a present back to his master and David is lying there and he is trying to go back to sleep but he can't and he comes and it's all happening again and then he falls asleep again.

'Good Morning, darling.'

David is blinking and it's the next morning and it's so early everything registers only as fragments. Broken pieces because he's trying to avoid putting it all together and facing the blotchy skinned red ringed reality.

'Tea without milk like you like.'

A plane leaves a vapour trail across the silent summer sky, tea steams up the melamine headboard. Mikey smokes, first thing in the morning it makes David feel terribly claustrophobic. The edges of two toweling gowns curl up like the pages of a well thumbed book, and fray in places like Shredded Wheat.

There are two head high mirrors on opposite sides of the bathroom which David jumps up and down between to check the progression of acne across his back and to make sure there are no lovebites on his bottom. There is much coughing and rattling teaspoons in cups and little bits floating in the bathwater and then David must go to work. Today is yesterday, tomorrow.

And I see Mikey and Paul in the pub tonight. The pub where they met David. But David's not really his name. Well, it might be. David's my name. I take the last cigarette out of the box out of my bag, stick it in my mouth and chuck my bag on to my shoulder.

ID: MORRIGAN : SSA 250A

PWR16
<OBGY>31.12m96
10:29:33
3.8CM
C3.75
19HZ

THE PROMISE

3/0/2
60/ 82
13.0CM

SHE TOLD ME ABOUT PERIODS AND
PENISES

P
E
N
I
S
E
S

SHE SAID THINGS ABOUT VAGINAS
AND VULVAS.

I was walking on the pavement, following the cracks in the paving slabs with mine eyes, soft strips of mossy cushions between grey marl squares.

She was pregnant, swollen and bulbous, "A hot air balloon in full flight," he said. I thought she looked like a tomato in that red dress.

There were green railings around the concrete playground to keep the cars and perverts out and the children in. When I touched Carol's cunt, when we were huddled under our coats by the logs set in concrete in the playground, at playtime, when I touched her cunt my fingers smelled of fried onions and garlic.

Why did he HIT TTT her

her

her

because she gave her boyfriend a biggah Easter egg than the one she gave him???????????????????? The table was oak and all the varnish had worn off the top where she scrubbed it with bleach. I traced the lines of the grains of the wood with my fingernail as he raged.

He smelled of distilled malt and had budgie shit on his shoulder. He said she had to have long hair because men like long hair, big bums and melonic tits. He liked long hair, big bums and melonic tits. He liked her long hair.

She was his daughter and she should have got him the biggest Easter egg.

Offerings to the altar and "Forgive me Father for I have sinned."

Forgive me Father for I have seen.

"Smile at the camera," he said, "Take your hands out of your mouth," he said, "Don't bloody mutter," he said. He said she had bled to death. He said "Work makes you free." He said "They should all be rounded up in a field and shot." Bodies on top of bodies ontopofbodiesontopofbodies piled into trenches, limbs sticking out at obscene angles, twisted corpses and naked pudendas.

He said I was "A nasty piece of work," kneeling in front of me as I sat in the brown chair with the cloth cover. He spat his words at me, his drying saliva whitening the corner cracks of his lips as I breathed second hand his cigarette breath.

She gave me a purple plastic packet of sanitary towels with peel-off paper tapes on the back that revealed a strip of shiny adhesive. I put the packet in my bedside cabinet drawer.

Sometimes she'd scrat t t ch at her pUbic hair through her clothes. Big browned hands with hoofy nails. She had a ring with a pearl set in erect white gold and surrounded by diamonds. She scratched through her nylon white corset with the embossed rose pattern and the yellow gusset. Her pUbic hair had thinned over the years, pale brown scatters, furrows of barren fuckundity. Sagging cunt sacks, flapping labia and an arsehole tagged with empty pile flesh.

She would check my small puckered arsehole for worms, white wiggly worms, the sort that live up your bum and in all the tubes and pipes in your tummy. I picked at my bottom too much. I liked to push my middle finger through the ring, feel the rim, the lip of tightness. I liked to sniff at my fingers, musty musky bum hole smell. My fingers smelled the same when I touched Carol.

I would think about Carol when I was face down on my bed, face in the scratchy blankets, my pillow gripped between my thighs, folded in two to make an extra pointy end which pressed into my porcelain clitoris. I didn't know I had a clitoris. She didn't tell me the word.

MY CLITORIS WAS UNNAMED
AND THEREFORE NON-EXISTENT.

MASTURBATION WAS UNNAMED
AND THEREFORE NON-EXISTENT.

ORGASM WAS UNNAMED
AND THEREFORE NON-EXISTENT.

One day, as I lay hunched on my bed, my pillow clasped between my legs, she opened my bedroom door and came in.

She sat on my bed and was revolted by me. I was shamed. She asked me what I was doing and I didn't know because I didn't have any words but I knew I was guilty.

I used to think about a boy in my class at school. He had ginger hair and I would come thinking about him busying into a nappy. Say 'busy' over and over, the word tastes of faecal matter. We didn't say pooh or crap, those words fall out of your mouth too easily, they can be spoken and discharged, but 'busy' fills your mouth with silt and durge, it is like the word diesel, it permeates into taste.

SAY THE WORDS PENIS,
VAGINA AND VULVA,

SAY SEXUAL INTERCOURSE.

SAY THEM WHEN YOU ARE 10,
SAY THEM WHEN YOU ARE 16,
SAY THEM WHEN YOU ARE 25,

Say them when you are 28 and grieve with the frustration of shame and filth. Stand above him as he lies on the rug. Stand with your skirts knotted around your thighs. Move between your cunt lips with your green pointed fingernails. Watch his squinted approval and the reflection of your cunt in his glasses.

My breasts didn't grow. I knew I was changing, she knew I was changing, she washed my bleached white knickers. She said my discharge was thickening. It left white scales on the fabric of my underwear. I would sit in the locked bathroom with the sky blue 'suite' and 'low flush WC' and the bidet for constant washing, and rub at the stained fabric, picking the flakes of dried discharge from my stiff gusset. It smelled bitter and sour when it was dry. I never washed my hands after. I would suck and bite at my nails, devouring the flakes that I teased out with my teeth.

I was fourteen and a half precisely, to the very day. I got up and went to the toilet. It was early morning and the sun didn't shine through the opaque dimpled bathroom window first thing. I wiped myself with tissue paper, back to front, legs bent and parted. I looked at the tissue paper and there was a soak of blood seeping around the finger mounds.

My mother was asleep.

My father was 8,000 miles away.

I remembered the purple packet of sanitary towels in my bedside cabinet. I went and got one. I was sweating. I peeled off the white paper strip decorated with pale blue writing. I stuffed the wodge into the gusset of a clean pair of knickers. The ones I had worn in bed the night before had brown stains that crusted around the edge of the gusset. I put them in a plastic bag and hid them in my school satchel and stuffed it in the built in wardrobe with the mahogany veneer doors and brass handles.

I went out.

I came back.

ID:

My periods weren't very regular.
I didn't have another one for six months.
I told no-one.
I hid each pair of filthy soiled knickers. After a year I had a wardrobe full of blood stained knickers.

One day I came home from school and she was sitting on my bed. I went into my room. She hit me so hard that my head smashed into the door jam. Her pearl ring with the diamonds cracked my cheekbone and bruised the socket of my eye. She had found my stash of knickers. She had then taken my bedroom apart, bit by bit, and found my notebooks, my fantastic scribblings about hard cocks and tonguey kisses, [WORDS]. She was dis Gusted. Her torrent of abuse lashed from her mouth. I had behaved like an animal, a bitch on heat. I am filthy. I am revolting, repulsive. I am humiliated and degraded. I am a fetid rotting mass of corruption. There is vomit and clawing. I scratch myself to gouge out the demon spawn, the chasms of infected blood pumps through my veins and spews into my brain myfuckingbrain.

FORGIVE ME FATHER FOR
I HAVE SINNED.

FORGIVE ME FATHER FOR
I HAVE SEEN.

At school they asked about my battered face. I told them my mother had done it. They asked what had I done to make her do that to me. I was mute. They said I was resistant to authority, a troublemaker, sarcastic and uncooperative. They did nothing.

I AM GUILTY. And I got used to having blood on my hands and fear in my guts.

At the clinic the windows were blacked out. Grey lino with black scuffs and not enough chairs to sit on. Mostly, they weren't women yet, they still staggered in their high heels and had flanks like unbroken colts. They were unconscious for the procedure, faces slack, the frowning worry lines slipped off their foreheads and into their dreams. With their legs in stirrups, flat on their backs, they look like plucked chickens being stuffed, their cold white flesh dimpled like the skin of a raw chicken carcass.

The first day I cleaned and moved

equipment around. The second day they asked me to help in theatre. I don't recall the patients, the penetrated and violated. Unconscious. Etiquette was not required here. Nameless. They were hollow, scooped out. The nurse, she had hair that hung in greying ragged rats' tails around her shoulders, her breath smelled of nicotine. She wore a spattered gown and latex gloves snapped around her veined wrists, her fat and flesh spilled out over the rim of her gloves puckering the white inside of her arm skin.

The foetuses were suctioned out through tubes. Sometimes the vacuum pump didn't work too well and the doctor would close his lips around the end of the tube and gently suck to get everything going. My dad used to do the same thing when he was draining sump oil or brake fluid. The remains of conception were slung into kidney shaped metal dishes. The nurse would inspect each abortion, squishing bloody corpuscles through her fingers. The bowls were emptied into the stainless steel sink. One sink, many remains. The women were wheeled in and out and in and out, all morning, all mourning, in and out, and the door would scrape against the floor where it had warped and needed a sixteenth of an inch shaved off the bottom.

When mourning theatre was over there was a mass of remains in the sink, soft crimson clots threaded with vermilion veins, starkly contrasted with the steel and the ringed industrial ridges of the moulded sink. The nurse was talking to me as we cleaned the area with disinfectant so strong it stripped the lining from my nostrils. She was talking and I couldn't hear what she was saying. She had her hand in the sink, one gloved hand clutching a biro she was jabbing at the plug hole, the circle symmetrically divided into segments, stabbing at the mass that obscured the hole, breaking it up with the tip of the ball point pen while she bit into an unbuttered cracker held in her other hand. I stifled the vomit.

And when I was pregnant, every morning, my mouth filled with saliva and I fought to keep my guts down. One day I was sick in the street and an old man hit me with his umbrella. He was red in the face and swearing at me as I hunched into the gutter. He was shouting that I shouldn't be drunk at this time in the morning. I said nothing as I repeatedly spat the stretched saliva of post vomit into the road.

I ran downstairs to the toilet, the low pulling pain in my fleshy pelvis was spasming into my legs. I knew there was something wrong.

I palmed my belly through the fabric of my clothes. Pleasepleasepleaseplease, please don't let this be happening. Forgive me Father.

My face was hot. I sat on the toilet and felt a warm flow, I felt the lumpy clots pass out of me and I heard them hit the water. I put my hand between my legs and felt the viscose blood on my fingers. I looked at my hand, the palm creases and cracks under my fingernails were stained arterial red. I wiped myself and the blood soaked along the ridges of my finger mounds.

In hospital they left me in a casualty cubical. The pissed old man next door was vomiting onto the green grey floor tiles and sometimes spatters of his sick would splash under the pastel floral curtains. They said there was nothing I could do. I lay on the cot in a white gown, a square of plastic backed cotton soaked up the endless blood flow. They said if I was going to miscarry there was nothing they could do. I tried to talk to her, I told her that I loved her and I didn't want her to go away. I hadn't chosen a name for her yet.

I had seen her on the scan, they had given me a picture of her, I had seen her moving inside me, but I hadn't given her a name. My lover wasn't there. I was alone and I was frantically searching for her name. I had to give her a name before she died. Without a name she would be nothing, she would be the remains of conception they would scrape out of my unconscious cleaved body. I couldn't find

a name. I lay on the cot with my hands on my belly, tears trapped in my eye sockets, saying over and over 'my baby, my baby, my baby'.

No-one came and the words morphed into autotoxicity and became strangled screams reverberating in the hollow vortex of my within that erased vision and sensation.

Six months later, at the end of Summer, in the middle of the night, when all was dark and still, I birthed her slithering body into her father's hands. Afterwards, I sat on our bed drinking sweet tea and eating grainy bread smothered in honey as he massaged jasmine oil into my shoulders. Her lust for life bellowed from her lungs as, blindly, her open mouth searched for my nipple.

And today, I watch her in the park. The boy with the ginger hair takes her little red bucket and she says nothing. She has no words as yet. She points and follows him to the sandpit in a legs wide open waddle. But the sandpit is enclosed by logs driven into concrete and she is too small to climb over. She staggers back to where I am sitting, drinking tea out of a polystyrene cup, and pats my leg with her fat hand. We go to the sandpit together and I lift her over the barrier.

We sit in the damp sand and I make sandcastles while she squeezes the sticky grains between her fingers. She trusts me. I am her mother and before her I didn't exist. 'Raven,' I say her name softly and she looks and smiles. Raven, the guise of the Morrigu as she sat on Cuchulain's shoulder and watched the beavers eat his entrails and drink his blood.

Raven, we are both daughters, you have pulled my past into my present and together we cast circles.

Published autumn 1999

SPACEHOPPER

price 7.99

ANNA LANDUCCI

POST HUMAN

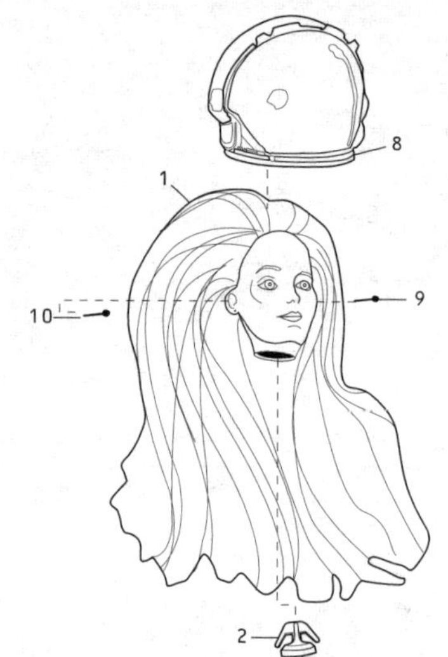

I'M NOT A REAL PERSON
I'VE MADE MYSELF UP
FROM ALL THE BEST BITS
OF PEOPLE I LIKED.
I'VE NICKED BITS FROM
GLOSSY MAGAZINES TOO--
ALL THOSE STAR
QUALITIES
THAT CROWDS LOVE SO.

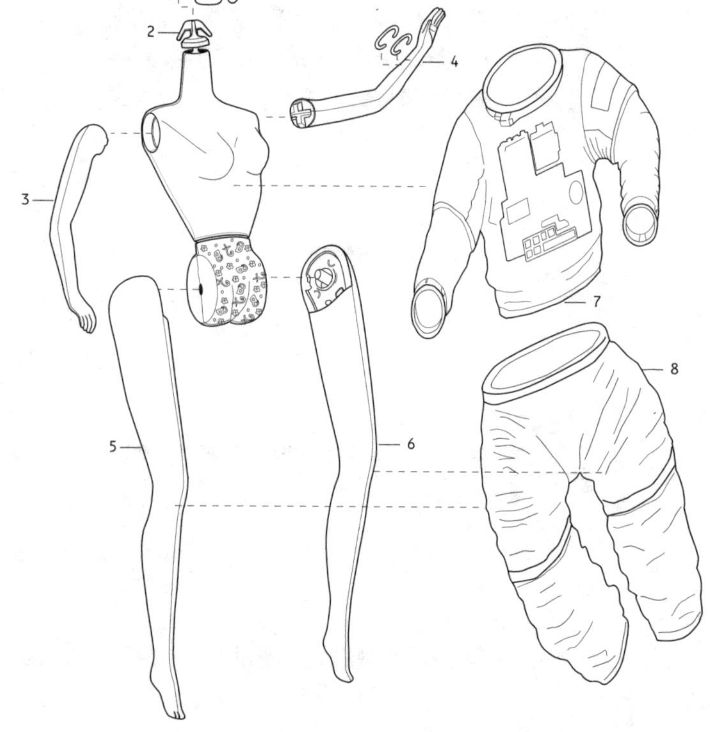

Stealing identities to make my own,
reinvented to survive the twenty first century.

A fabulous invention of one
Into hyper space--the future is mine
Is this the end of the world?
Is it anything like what was predicted?
You can't touch me because I'm not real--
Barbie perfect--plastic perfect--yes wrapped in
cellophane to protect me from the journey.

I've brainwashed away those annoying things that
society programmes in, so I can be virgin for
the next 100 years.
Impressed by electronic dreams. Speed is my
swipe card, forget the rockets--
I'm leaving you behind.
I'm fed up with hanging around this sad century.
Leaving for an irresistible planet that keeps me
more fascinated than earth, that you can gauge
in light years. I'm happy, I'm going to chill
with some cool aliens.
So go join your own cult, I'm busy packing for
my new life because I'm post human, beyond
nature.

On day zero I begin again.
On the last midnight of the century I'll see you
to say goodbye.

JUMP

by Sparky

He couldn't believe it when she jumped.
High on the ledge.
One minute she was there and the next gone.
Just like that.

All day she had been depressed. As the tears formed he knew she was on her way to a better place.

'Hey honey, whats up?' he'd asked over breakfast.

'Nothing,' she whispered, head full of clouds.
'Just wanna get high.'

But they had to wait. First thing you learn is that you always gotta wait. Kathy was 'the man'—she had thrown them into it. Older, wiser,she had come to them—'Yesterday I was so high! I mean, really out there! Soooo good!' she pushed the words out between breathless breaths, freeing their minds by capturing their desire. That was the beginning of the fall.

He had loved Kathy, but now Alice was the only. For a time, all three of them enjoyed the rush together. Until last week when Kathy ran herself into the ground. His last memory was her smile, uncertain and faded. Last night in a dream, an angel who had come to protect him lost its wings and fell to earth.

'I miss her so much!' It hit Alice hardest. Her perfectly packed backpack was now ripped and torn inside. She just didn't want to think any more. More than ever now, she needed the pure thrill of the rush to cover the pain. Her dream was spiraling toward the ground with zero resistance.

We knew we had to end it. We both knew that this had to be the last time. The risks were too high. Maybe we would be able to pull through. Maybe this time we would hit the ground running. It all seemed so different from up here. Up here everything that was difficult became easy. The door was open, you just had to choose whether to go through or whether to stay behind.

So they had gone to the usual place and gone through the ritual. Pretty soon they were floating high above the world. Somewhere between reality and fantasy he woke from a dream.

And then she was on the ledge. He didn't think she would do it. Really, really didn't think she'd be able to do it. And then, suddenly out of time, she jumped and was gone. Just like that.

He ran to the ledge screaming and screaming and then he jumped. As the wind pushed his face to terminal velocity he could see the island and Alice's open 'chute way below. He let gravity take control and enjoyed the ride.

SPLIT

Nik Houghton

YOU'RE GOING NOWHERE FAST. YOU'RE FALLING APART SLOWLY YOU'RE SLIPPING DOWN. OH, YES. YES YOU ARE.

You come home from another slow day at work to the usual stuff. Another numbed out night, another TV evening, a few cans, a couple of king-kong spliffs to get you through. What are you living for exactly?

Got some news? Well...Yeah! Grand-daddy died and there's a little cash coming your way. How much? A few thou. Enough.

You're going to do it properly now. You're going into the fast lane. You've been idling in some backstreet for a while but now you're headed for a dark place. It's in your heart.

You've dabbled of course: those joyriding nights, the stonefire days with the bad boys and that time when you chased the dragon, tasted the smacked out euphoria...Oh, yeah. Take me back there. I don't belong here.

(Really. Truly).

You lay your plans while you wait for the money. You define your territory. You've had enough of the office coffee and strategy implementations, broken photocopiers and departmental memoes. You've got other things to do now.

Easy: The cheque comes and a week later you're out of work, out of your head, in luck and geared up. Go for it.

DAY ONE – You're smoking the big H with a gangly punk called Clinch in a fire-damaged squat up Highbury way. You're nodded and toned-down, feeling freefall fine.

"I want a gun," you tell Clinch. (Do you? Really? Where did that idea come from? Is it the skag kicking loose some real need, a darkheart impulse?) Clinch is in a smiley half doze, starting to dribble. "Oh, yeah...Right...Right...Yeah, a shooter...A pop-pop gun." He giggles, reaches for a cigarete. "A pistol...A sex pistol."

Head home in your car in a sickly dawn light. The day is bleached grey and you feel sick and grizzled. Get home. Get home...You spend the AM drinking hot tea, eating biscuits for breakfast, chewing cigarettes and rolling skanky joints until you're muzzed out and close to sleep. This is the start, you think, as you slip into dingy dreams.

DAY FOUR – Wired and wicked, looped and lurching and you're clenched tight with nerves, tickled with fear, buzzed with high grade amphetamines.

The car park is bareboned and skeletal in the 2AM quiet.

You sit in your car listening to techno, eyes scanning the concrete driveways and parking bays. They are already 30 minutes late. A battered Ford hatchback prowls up the ramps and idles in Bay 66. A bulky man, cut price leather jacket, drooping jogger pants, a grey ponytail, gets out of the car and lopes across.

You get out of your car and, close up, smell his sweat as he nods hello.

"You want some help?" The man has pocked and yellowing skin, a bad shaving cut on his jowls that you can't stop staring at.

"Yes. Back of the motor."

The boot of the Ford contains a box of unmarked video tapes and a canvas holdall. The man unzips the holdall with a slow theatrical gesture. Inside, see-through ziplock bags contain handguns and ammo, an Uzi, a sawn-off...Sexy.

You pays yer money and you takes yer pick, drive home suddenly exhausted and relieved. Back home you can't sleep, the spiky ghost of a chemical high keeping you awake. At 5AM you drink half a bottle of Benylin, swallow two Temazepam, and float into a murked and melting sleep.

DAY TEN – She's fucking you h-a-a-a-r-r-d and it almost hurts the way she humps and grinds. But your cock is stiff and she's juiced up and high on sexstuff. Hands curl and clutch at grimy sheets. You think you might pass out/throw up/go weird. She is somewhere else, eyes closed, pulling at her breasts, plucking at the nipplenubs, one hand on her own belly, palm pressed down.

"Come onnnn...Come ON."

You're not there, bot. You're not in her universe. Oooh, no.

You're just d-i-c-k. Something to fuck. So...DO IT.

She's a wild girrrl with her biker boots and attitude, out on the prowl. A heartbreaker looking for a quick fuck. He'll do.

"Come on......come onnnn." She punches her lips forward, cunt clutching his cock. He feels like his prick is being wrenched out by its roots. She gives a she-wolf growl as she comes, shudders, tugs at her titty-tips and pushes a sticky finger into his mouth. "Hmmm...Lovely."

He goes soft, feels lost. Sjhe hasn't even asked his name, hasn't kissed him yet. She gives her clit a little rub, reaches underneath for his balls.

"No spunky?"

"No."

"Nevermind...Later."

She pulls free, flops, reaches for cigarettes. "You're OK," she says, lighting up two smokes, passing him one.

He smiles weakly, sucks smoke into his lung, the reassuring ritual of tobacco. He wants to get out/wants her to hold him/wants to fuck her again.

"You want to do this again sometime?" she says, fingertip stroking his ball bag.

DAY THIRTEEN – You lie in bed most of the day crapped out from a 2 day speed binge and too much booze. You have blurred memories of a dawn drive to Brixton, a hi-rise deal and a skeleton selling you pills and powders, an armoury of uppers, downers, twisters. Stuff to make you fly. Dusts to make you holy. Tonic for the tired mind.

Remember her touch on your body-cock, mouth, nipple, teeth?

Remember the smell of hunger sex?

Towards early evening you take a bath, shave, pull on some clean clothes and chew some hot food.

What next, big boy?

In the wastelands of the Docks zone you find an empty warehouse, dirty river water slapping at the dead stone, and pop off some shots. The pistol kicks hard, gives out a flat, fat noise. It feels good.

LATER – You prowl the empty streets. Are you big enough for all this? Is this what you've been looking for all of your sad, sickly life?

You get drunk in a Whitechapel boozer, something surging under your skin, something ticking in your heart, drive home to watch porno and smoke yourself giggly on skunkweed.

DAY FIFTEEN – A back street club close to midnight. She's with you, double sexy in those black leggings, putting out voodoo vibes. "You're alright," she says. "I like you...You're strange."

There's a grunge guitar outfit getting feedback funky onstage. She knows the band, grins. "I've fucked her...and him," she says, pointing. "Oh yeah," you say.

It's too loud, too hot, too busy in here. You can't forget the big kick on the pistol, the gun, the flatflatslap of that sexpistol. You want to tell her. You want to put your hand on her ass and stroke her cunt. You want to... The coke kicks in bigtime and your bones seem to expand. The music sounds good.

And later she smells of new sweat and tastes of salt swamps, fucks like a baby tiger. Mouth to mouth, his hands on her ass, pulling, pushing, poking...ohh yeah, do that, go on gunboy, do it good. He comes crackerjack style. Yummy.

DAY SIXTEEN – Iggy Pop on the cassette player and rolling through Aldgate midday. There was a time when you'd be working at this time of the day, waiting for lunch, slipping towards another afternoon. But not now. That was someone else. That was another time. That was before the split.

DAY SEVENTEEN – Weird day. Strange. Today you only smoke cigarettes, drink only tea and water. Your head clears though your body feels heavy. You go for a walk by the canal and are surprised by the weight of the still water, the noise of a blackbird...Weird.

DAY TWENTY-FIVE –

1.45AM – Crack smoke in a chintzy Peckham council flat with a man called Diz who talks incessantly about fucking schoolgirls.

2.55AM – Docklands: Popping shots across the water until a car headlight flares behind you. Freeze. Sidle through the rubble and skippety-hop to your car.

4.10AM – Tea and spliff doctored with a smear of opium. Spinhead. Hard on.

5.30AM – Mushy morning. At the bogside spilling a drool of green bile onto the china.

6.10AM – When will sleep come? Pop sleepers and drift while someone whispers 'Sex pistols...Sex pistol.'

DREAMTIME – Figures floating and she's on her back, legs open, riding a dildo-gun.

11.05AM – Tea and toast. Build a 5-skinner and kickback.

12.30PM – Drive to her squat. Gary, spotty, fifty and dreadlocked answers the door. (He says he's 'black in soul,' though he's pasty white skinned, lumpy and dumb). She is upstairs, slumped in bed. Slip into bed and rub those titties, work that slit. She comes. Little moaner. "Oooh......He-LLO!"

1.25PM – Limp dick. Sniff coke off her belly. She hums with wimmin energy. She finds herself a vibrator. Does herself a favour. Watch close, gunboy, little man.

1.55PM – Dribble spunk. She licks it up.

2.30PM – Tea and hot food in 'Franck'. She reads a book, says "Get some sleep, you look like shit."

3.15PM – Notting Hill boozer with Mickey, ratfaced and rundown. Bottles of fizz.

4.15PM – Mickey is smacked up and sleepy on a dumpy sofa. There is hardcore on the video and you think of the gun and smoke H until you're spacey, soft and sinking into the carpet.

9PM – Have to stop on the drive home to heave.

9.55PM – Brush your teeth three times. Drink instant coffee and chew biscuits and notice the spots on your shoulder and feel a buzzbomb headache building and God you feel so, so tired and weary and wouldn't it be good to fall asleep and wake up with her. Think Don't blow it gunboy, bigboy. Don't back down now. It's just getting good.

11.20PM – Those lonely planet boy blues in a Stokey punk pub. Dog people in army fatigues and pierced splendour sprawl and booze and you drink heavy, takes toots of gritty speed in the toilet cubicle, chain triple twitchy. And a voice is saying: Go faster, gunman, pistol-boy.Step sharp, shooter.

12.05AM – Where did she come from? Who is she? You're in a grunged-up room somewhere with a dog girl and you're fucking but you don't know why and the TV is on and there's Sonic Youth playing somewhere and this woman is thrashing and you feel like a robot... And then it's dark and cold and you wake up in your car.It is 3AM.

DAY THIRTY FIVE – Pop-pop-pop across the canal wasteland. Pop-pop-pop. Do you feel better now big man, gunboy, sex-pistol?

DAY THIRTY SEVEN – The trouble starts in a Poplar Pub. You're there with Her, though she's distant and quiet, wary. Beery boys give her the eye, shoot hardman glances, come and sit at your table. "That your girlfriend? Do you fuck her?" You stare at them and something happens—you split into two. And one part of you looks on as another part takes over. This is your destiny, then. This is maybe the point.

You smile. "Fuck off." The beery boys look confused. "What?" Don't wait. GO. Across the table, clumsy but intent. Snapshots. The torn leather of the guy's jacket as he goes down.

The sole of a boot as it hits you in the face. The soundtrack playing in the bar. Her shout. A fist in the face. You're going wobbly. A grunt as the third one lashes, connects, knocks you over. And then—absolute quiet. Perfect peace for just a moment until the clamour starts again. Voices and bodies and you're being hauled out into the night. "Come on," she says, "let's go."

You're close to the car when they spot you and come running. It's OK. You move slow and careful and ease the pop-pop from under the driver's seat. Lock the firing. Hold her steady.

The first one comes at full tilt, bleach white face, rat-eyed in the bad yellow light. "Come on, you cunt...You fucking—"

Swing the gun up. Beer boy cannot believe it. (He does not understand.) He is like an animal faced with something new. It is not fair. It's not supposed to be like this. Blap. Blap. Blap. Two shots take him off his feet. The two others skid to a stop.

You move quickly. Do not run but walk fast. Everything seems to come together now, everything seems in place.

No 2 has ducked into a doorway. He is bulky, ugly, says "Don't." Blap. He's neckshot and surprised. Blood pumps yards. Blap. Headshot. He twitches to death.

Now...Where is the other one?

Something moves behind a car. Somewhere very distant there is a lot of shouting. (Is this enough gunboy? Have you tasted enough yet? Is the hunger gone?) No 3 is slippy, slinky, tumbles between cars. Blap. A windscreen shatters.

You crouch to slot in a new magazine. Light headed but certain of things. No 3 makes a break and you swivel, wing him, fire again. Blap. Behind you someone running. Twist and fire. Twist back and blap-blap takes down No 3 dead.

As you turn you feel so-so high. So strange and light.

You walk back to the car and see she is lying on her side.

There is a hole in her face.

At home you wash your hands and face in scalding water. You collect your dusts and tonics, pills and liquids and set them carefully on the table.

Time has stopped. You feel calm. You start your work, carefully chop a line and load a syginge, pour out a glass of water.

Time to split.

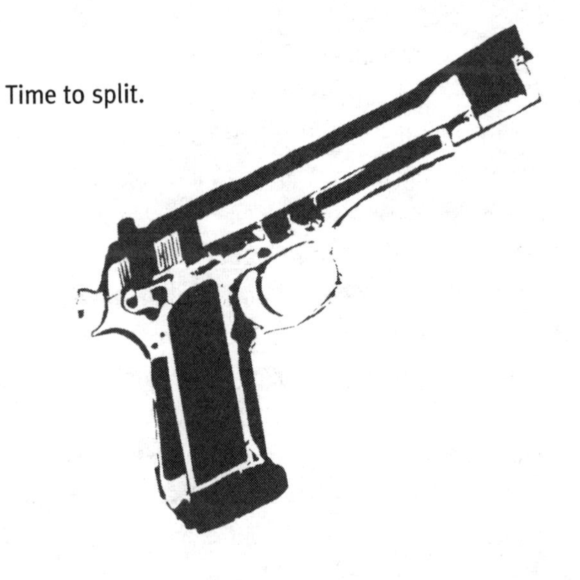

NO TIME FOR ICE CREAM

IAN CUSACK

Just before Easter, Maria had started telling everyone that she'd finally kicked me out. Of course I denied it and said I'd left her, even though no-one believed me. Least of all Chris, who'd loaned me his sofa for a couple of nights and still had me hanging around three weeks later. The daft thing was everyone had known we were going to split, but us. Arguments in bars, the bedroom window going through at three in the morning, that sort of thing. People aren't stupid. When she finally gave me my marching orders after one slanging match too many, all I took was a suitcase full of clothes and half a dozen albums. My favourites: Velvet Underground & Nico, Kind Of Blue, the sort of stuff she hated.

Without Maria, I was forever at a loose end. I couldn't hang around Chris's flat every night. Sometimes I made us a meal and we got loaded together, but mostly I went down Paul's Bar, got pissed and acted miserable. Word got round that Maria was drinking in The Anchor over in Portstewart and seeing someone else; Terry, a big guy from the country who drove a bread lorry and shipped tack to Kilrea and Cookstown. I hadn't the heart to go over there and cause a scene so I concentrated on the pints.

One Thursday night, a few of us went to The Derry to see some indie band. They were shit: all cover versions and broken strings, so we grabbed a table in the back room away from the noise. About half twelve, Maria came in with a couple of the girls she'd always hung out with, but not Terry. Of course she darted back to the main room when she saw me.

I played it calm, sat still, didn't race over offering to eat her shit off a spoon, but two drinks later and a mile more miserable, I was ready to have it out with her. I'd intended asking when I could get my stuff back, then quitting the conversation whilst I was ahead. I could always turn on the sob story when I got round there. Trouble was, everything I said came out wrong, like I was spoiling for an argument. It ended up as a screaming match that drowned out the band. The whole place was watching us, anticipating a fight. So we had one.

She called me a loser and I called her a whore and then she stubbed a fag out on my right cheek.

Fuck me, it hurt. I never realised a burn could sting so much and I swear it was just a reflex when, seconds later, I floored Maria with a left hook, flush on the chin. The place exploded, girls showered me with drinks and spit, scrabbling at my face with their nails. Two bouncers hauled me outside. They didn't give me a kicking or anything, just told me to fuck off. Her mates stood around the entrance, threatening to have me lifted or shot.

It was round about then I accepted that me and Maria were probably history. Maybe if that last fight in the flat had been a proper battle, maybe if she'd thrown all my stuff out on to Causeway Street, I'd have got things sorted in my head a bit quicker. I went back to Paul's Bar and bought a carry out, then sat by the harbour, waiting for the cops or Terry. No-one turned up, so I finished the cans and started walking home, back along the train line. Watched the moon's reflection in the receding Atlantic. I knew I'd never ice skate, drunk, at three in the morning down Strand Road with Maria again.

Spring was cold that year. Frost whitened the pavements and exhaled breath was a vapour during Holy Week. Barry's Fun Fair opened for the holidays and was deserted. Chris had started seeing Roisín who worked the refreshments stall, so he took me up there for free ice creams. She shivered in the wooden booth with only Silk Cut for company. The cornets she gave us wouldn't melt and my teeth ached in the biting wind.

For weeks I'd wanted to leave this freezing paradise. I was unsettled. The business with Maria had bruised my spirit. It hadn't been a divorce, strictly speaking, but it was the closest thing to one I'd ever come. Chris had been good, putting me up, but his landlord was a bastard. I'd got one last month on his settee and after that I'd be homeless. Just in time for Summer, when the students leave and the tourists arrive. Three months of Shankhill On Sea. Fuck that. I'd spent four years lying around, drinking beer, smoking tack and arguing with Maria, punctuated only by the odd spell working in Liam's second-hand record shop. A change had to come.

On Good Friday a gang of us, migrants home for the long weekend all bringing London with them, and some of us local layabouts, sat late in Paul's Bar. The talk was of twelve inch dance records and designer gear, of coke and opiated black that was cheaper than the home grown we survived on. At closing time a few of us went back to Roisín's with some cans. People started drifting away, but I listened intently to John's stories of regular work and English women. He had money, smart clothes, a flat and his accent had changed. By the end of the night the usual drunken offers of spare rooms and jobs were flying around. There were beds in Belsize Park, Ladbroke Grove, Notting Hill. Small enclaves of the capital that would be forever Portrush.

Around four o'clock I left alone, the last guest. Chris and Roisin had gone to bed hours ago and John was crashed out on the floor, still cuddling a litre of screw-top red. The streets were deserted as I walked back, facefuls of wind checking my progress. I changed a whimper into a cough as I felt tears cluster round my eyelids. In the flat, I lay out on the settee, drinking the dregs of my carry-out and listened to Rum, Sodomy & The Lash twice, straight through.

On Saturday I stayed in. Scared that if I got pissed I'd take John up on his offer of somewhere to crash and find myself signing on in Westbourne Park next week. I weighed up the options over endless black coffees and half an ounce of Golden Virginia.

Late Sunday morning I met John on Lansdowne Crescent. He looked rough, eyes shot to shit. He'd been on the rip the day before and had ended up at some party way out past the golf club. I was heading up to my mother's for dinner, so I invited him along. She always welcomed another mouth to feed, except when it used to be Maria.

As it turned out, there were only two of us to keep Mam company. Every Easter Sunday she cooked a big turkey and the family let her down. My sister had stayed home with her kids and my brother was in Holland. Me and John had to stuff ourselves. It would have been rude to be picky. Afterwards, I dozed in front of the TV while John got the third degree, Mam wanting to know why he lived over there and telling him what an awful place London was, though she'd never been. The same shit I'd heard for years. It always got me down, made me feel guilty for staying. John started to get uncomfortable, shooting me tense glances.

When we left, Mam followed us to the door, asking when I'd be round with my washing, whether I'd got my stuff back from *her*. (She still wouldn't use Maria's name, or accept that maybe I'd been in the wrong.) Halfway down the garden path I turned.

"I'm off to London tomorrow. John's got a spare bed and they reckon work's easy to get."

Right then, that very second, I'd decided to leave. I half expected her to cry, or start giving out, but she just looked blank. Her voice, when it came, sounded wooden. "Please yourself." That tone of voice always pissed me off. Injured innocence. I thought about giving her a kiss or a hug, but couldn't. Not in front of John.

I only smiled when she went back in and closed the door.

Me and John hit Paul's Bar around half seven. We were in for the night, drinking Guinness with brandy chasers. John was paying. It felt like Christmas. A few others came in, fixing up lifts to Larne or checking on trains to Antrim for the airport. Everyone was going back to England. Including me this time. A guy from Dervock I hardly even knew promised he'd try and get me a start painting and decorating. At last orders, I blew the rest of my giro on pints and shorts for everyone. Someone proposed a toast to "The Paul's Bar Diaspora" and we all got to our feet and knocked back Tequilas in one. I thought I saw Maria at one point, but couldn't get round to see her before she left. Too many people.

It didn't take too long to pack next morning. One suitcase. Mainly clothes topped up with favourite tapes and some books I'd not got round to reading. I left the key and a note for Chris, promising to send him a few quid when I got straight. Opening the door, I noticed an envelope wedged in the letterbox. It was a card from Mam: I'll miss you. Phone when you've a minute. She'd stuck in a hundred quid as well. Fresh notes, straight out the machine.

I shut the door behind me and stood looking out past Barry's and on to the rest of the town. It was raining heavy. I turned my collar up and hurried for the train.

LADYBOYS
OF
KOH
SAMUI
BEE

'I don't know why the fuck we had to hire a motorbike,' I snarled.

'Because it's the only way to get around the island at night,' mumbled Flange.

The bike screeched like a spoilt child.

'Well I can't get my head around these fuckin' gears.'

'OK I'll drive,' said Flange.

After a short bumpy ride I felt calmer. We pulled up outside the local disco. Fashioned from bamboo splattered with UV paint, nestling between giant palm trees, it looked like a tripped out tree house. Flange parked the bike and switched the lights on. I said that it might have been better to have had the lights on when we were actually on the road. She sniggered, bent down in front of the beam with a hand mirror and sorted out the lipstick which had crept onto her teeth.

I went inside and ordered the usual bottle of Mekong whiskey, soda, ice and packet of Krung Thip cigarettes. You don't have to worry about the nicotine in Krung Thips—it's safer than candy compared to the other chemicals in them.

The DJ was playing trashy music. We joined the other people sat outside on straw mats. I fixed the drinks. Our glasses clinked like swords as we said 'Chok Dee'.

I sipped and surveyed the garden, my lusty eyes drifting over each group of people like a hungry insect searching for its favourite flower.

Two drinks later I commented on the lack of cute guys.

'So I guess it's time for the Pooh Bear box,' Flange said, reaching into her waistband pocket and handing me a tiny egg-shaped tin with a smiling bear on the lid. I broke it open and gazed at the various uppers and downers which often

turned our insides out. My fingers hovered over the box, dowsing rods coming to rest above two Rohypnol tablets. I crushed them into our drinks, 'Going down, next floor street level.'

Earlier in the day we had both agreed that Koh Samui was the final resting place for those who have sunk to depths of depravity that god fearing people only read about in tabloids. The majority of tourists are fat middle aged men with little money and even less taste. They probably started their holiday sight-seeing around Bangkok's exotic temples, eating in good restaurants and staying in plush hotels. They nipped down the coast to Pattaya to get some sea air and blew most of their money getting blown by ladies of the night who disappeared early in the morning with their wallets. Having climaxed too quickly there's only two options left, home or Samui.

The prostitutes aren't much better looking. The only things which haven't changed over the years are their make-up, dress sense and dreams of dollars. Yup, Suzy Wong did not become an elderly lady who sits weaving and wondering about her misspent youth—she's still up there dancing on a podium in Samui.

Our favorite errant sister was Veena who would dance like a banshee on the bar. Black ski pants wobbling around like condoms full of KY. Big breasts spilling over her bra, worth their weight in silicone. Flange bought her a beer and got the story. She had moved down from Pattaya with her tatooist boyfriend. One drunken night she got him to tattoo her eyebrows. Being more drunk than she was, he hit upon the novel idea of signing his name, first and last over each eye. She got a screwed up face, he got a Singha beer bottle over the head.

On flat nights like this we missed Bangkok but as the Mekong Whisky and Rohypnol smoothed the edges, a blissful mood descended. Suddenly I saw my ship in the night sitting near us on the lawn. Let the Carnival begin...

'Is he looking?'

'He's 'orrible,' muttered Flange.

'Have you got your contacts in?' I asked.

'No, I left them in solution at the bungalow.'

'Well shut the fuck up then,' I squawked back.

'Besides,' I went on, 'you've done worse, only you were sober and he is looking at me.'

I raised a drunken eyebrow in the boy's direction, he smiled. Two raised eyebrows and he spoke.

'Hello where you come from?'

'England,' I replied.

He looked at Flange.

'This is my older sister,' I said hoping to untangle his puzzled brow.

'Younger, younger,' snapped Flange.

I motioned him to join us. Dispensing with formalities, he positioned himself on my lap and said, 'Tonight I sleep your room.'

Knowing how difficult it can be to get rid of people in the morning—it was of course strictly a casual encounter—I said, 'No, no my room too far, your room better.'

He smiled.

As I looked at him closely I began to think that maybe Flange was right. Several drinks later I didn't care. He suggested we left. I looked over at Flange: she had complained of dizziness ten minutes ago, put her head down on the straw mat and not surfaced since.

'She'll be OK here,' I said, thinking it would be a good excuse to come back once the deed was done. Unless of course, I did my usual trick and fell to sleep half way through the second act

probably waking up in the morning trying hard to remember where Flange was and more to the point where I was.

'Here, here,' he pointed as we approached a shabby block of apartments. The door of room 518 was covered in dirty finger marks, faded posters of Marilyn Monroe and scratched 'I Love Samui' stickers. He knocked three times which surprised me because Thais usually barge straight in. Our entrance was heralded by a fanfare of screeches from three Thai transvestites who were sat in their cheap lacy underwear on the tiny bed that filled the poky room. Thai Transvestites don't have a long shelf life and usually lose their looks mid twenties. These three were fast approaching forty.

They'll leave, I thought. They always do.

Simultaneously they all rose and moved towards me pulling each other back at the same time. The first one to reach me put her man sized hand round the back of my neck and pulled me towards her. The second one grabbed my shoulders and pulled me in the opposite direction. The third went straight for my crotch. I looked over at the boy who was now sat head in hands on the bed. I widened my eyes, gestured for help but his face had the look of a fisherman who had just lost his catch. I was on my own with the three ladyboys.

Their cackling grew louder, they ran their fat fingers through my hair, stroked my cheek and kneaded my crotch. The terror seem to mix well with the Thai whisky which flooded my veins and I was rooted to the floor. The room began to spin.

Haggard faces appeared like unwanted visions, drifting in and out of focus. A bull dog with electric blue eye shadow and crooked protruding teeth. A bull frog with slimy suction pump lips that muffled my cries for help and left trails of stringy saliva with each kiss. The third looked like her face had been hit by a bulldozer and stuck back together with Max Factor foundation. They each grabbed my hands and forced me to cup their oestrogen induced breasts, hoping I would give in to their manly/womanly charms. They only stopped mauling momentarily to inspect the labels of my clothes as each article was cast aside. Within seconds I stood shaking in a pair of loose fitting boxer shorts, six hands struggling to be the first inside the tiny slit to claim the shrivelled up prize. Only three buttons between it and them.

As the last button popped there was a loud knock on the door. They all froze like cartoons. An aggressive man's voice cut through the door like a chainsaw, getting louder as his knocking became fiercer.

Quicker than my clothes had been stripped they were flung haphazardly back on my quivering body and the door was opened. Stood there in all their glory were three policemen. They waltzed into the room but carried on shouting at the same level. They paid no attention to me or my dishevelled state, their scowling eyes looking straight through me. The door was still wide open. I was toying with the idea of bolting when suddenly the bullfrog turned to me:

'Is OK, OK darling, you wait here, we come back,' she hollered.

The police circled themselves around the pantyhose clad posse and herded them to one side.

The bull dog broke away momentarily to screech in my direction:

'Ok na! You wait here for me! Na!'

'Sure, I'll put the kettle on and make a brew, sweetheart,' I shouted at the group of squabbling trannys who were now being handcuffed to the boy.

I ran back to the disco where I found Flange asleep in the same place. I wondered why the police had turned up, but didn't get my answer until months later when I met the boy again in a Bangkok bar and he told me that they had been arrested for stealing a gold watch from a western trick.

Had it all been a bad dream, I wondered as I pulled her up, threw her on the back of the bike and drove off in third gear.

Martin Sketchley

PUPPY FAT

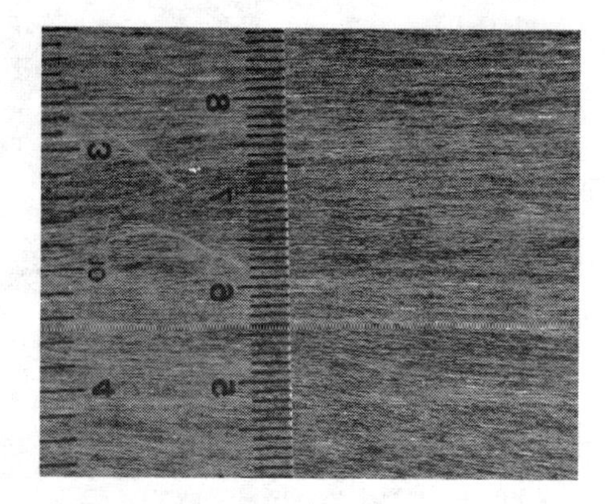

I sulked in my bedroom, insecurity winning again. I could hear the others downstairs in the living room though; laughing. No details, just long moments of silence followed by lots of noise. Mutant Walrus cartoons were stupid. I'd never noticed it before, but without the sound on, it was crap.

I really wanted to join in with the fun and games of course. Make jokes and be a part of it. I just pretended I didn't. If it had just been Mum, Dad, Sylvia and Jack, then maybe I would've gone down, poked my head around the door and smiled 'Hello'. But they had to go and bring Katie with them, so I couldn't.

I edged off the bed, went to the door and opened it slightly. Spoons were rattling cups so I strained to hear the fragments of conversation sharp enough to cut through.

'How's school, Katie?' my mum said.

Katie said something I couldn't hear, but I could see her in my mind, shrugging, peering through her fringe, blushing, and her usual 'all right, I s'pose'.

'She's been a bit depressed haven't you, love?' said Sylvia.

Boyfriend problems? I thought, even though I knew I'd have no chance even if...

'She reckons she's overweight,' continued Sylvia.

'No! I wish I was your weight, Katie.'

'I've tried to explain to her that it's just a bit of puppy fat. Just a stage she's going through. But you know what kids are like...'

'She's right, love. I don't know; you kids these days.'

Katie would be blushing hard and trying to make herself as small as possible as the conversation revolved around her. It happened to me too sometimes, being the only one.

My mum said, 'Yes, of course, love. You know where it is,' and there were steps on the stairs.

Scooping dirty boxers and socks beneath the bed, I hopped back on, careful to leave the door open just wide enough so I'd be visible from the landing. I lay on one side, propped up on my elbow, my back to the door. I was cool; relaxed; a youth with poise. This was my chance to make an impression.

Katie was sixteen; older, taller, wiser, more glandular and, if the rumours were true, had a six-foot boyfriend who could kiss without nearly knocking her teeth out. A boyfriend who stayed nights at her house. A boyfriend who called her mum, 'Sylvia', and her Dad, 'Jack'. A boyfriend with a motorbike. Sylvia had once told my mum that he was a Stallion. I heard them when they were in the kitchen. They'd giggled for about five minutes.

Katie was blonde, and I'd always fancied blondes. Even dodgy ones. Even blond men; the Bee Gees, David Soul. Apart from being blonde though, Katie also had breasts. I knew because I'd once seen her in the Co-op with her mum buying a bra. That surprised me because I'd never thought about it before. I'd been too embarrassed to stop and chat and have a closer look. I just blushed, kept my head down and walked on to the record department.

I glanced back to the landing: white polo shirt, jeans, Dunlop Green Flash pumps, breasts, blonde hair....

But she didn't look at me.

I turned the television up again, disappointed but not surprised. Mutant Walrus screamed something as he killed an evil creature by sticking a magical sword into it. It would not be cool, I thought, to be caught by someone with blonde hair and breasts watching cartoons that featured magical swords. I switched over to Blue Peter.

The toilet was right next to my bedroom, so I heard the flush even with the sound up. I tried hard to concentrate on the telly as the sound of the door unlocking echoed across the landing. But the tap on my bedroom door a few moments later made me jump.

I made myself look around slowly.

'Hi Steve,' said Katie, smiling.

I shuffled into a sort of sitting position. 'Er...hi, Katie. Come in.' I thought I could smell my own feet. I wished I'd washed my hair and brushed my teeth.

'Mind if I sit down?' she asked. 'They're doing my head in down there.' She looked around. 'Nice room.'

I smiled some sort of thanks and looked at my posters as if they were someone else's. But having a girl in my room was a new experience. Other guys at school made frequent claims of having had girls in their rooms but...

'I hate Blue Peter,' she said, sitting so close I could smell the fabric conditioner on her Polo shirt.

'Me too,' I said. 'Don't know why it's on.' I turned back to Mutant Walrus.

She began to pick through my record collection. She seemed impressed by Adam and the Ants and David Bowie, especially the old albums, but not so much by Shakin' Stevens. Every so often she'd say things like 'Oh my God!' and 'You never bought that!' I had lots of presents from my mum that day.

As she began to pore over my tapes, Sylvia called her.

'Come on, Katie, love. We're off now.'

'She's probably canoodling with Steve,' said Dad from the bottom of the stairs. I went red and thought if only, but Katie didn't seem to have heard.

'Can I borrow these?' she asked, holding up a stack of singles.

They were all my favourites and I wanted to say no but... 'Sure,' I shrugged. 'Give them back whenever.'

'Thanks, Steve. You're an angel.' She stepped forward and kissed my cheek, her chest brushing my arm. Then she slipped out of the room and went downstairs.

I examined my sleeve very closely.

Jack was a mate of Dad's from work. That's how they all met. He and Sylvia would come round to our house every other Saturday night for hot-dogs with onions, and we'd watch Doctor Who and The Generation Game. The other weeks it was our turn. We'd go around to their house, eat hot-dogs with onions and watch Doctor Who and The Generation Game. Sometimes I'd get to listen to some crap music on Jack's headphones. We didn't have headphones, so that made up for the music.

Dad always sat in the living room with Jack; they'd talk about football, lawn mowing and the women on The Generation Game. Mum and Sylvia, while cutting bread rolls and sniffing over the onions, talked about who'd recently become pregnant. There was rarely any sign of Katie. Sometimes she'd poke her head around the door to say 'see ya' as she went out, but that was about it.

My records weren't mentioned. I always wondered where she was going, what she'd be doing there, and who with. I once sneaked into her bedroom after I'd been to the toilet. It smelt like warm washing. She had posters of Spandau Ballet on her walls and flowery curtains. It was another world. Girls' lives seemed so completely different. No dirty underpants or socks. No hidden pictures of naked women. No stains on the sheets. Underwear washed every day, no matter what. A book lay on the dressing table next to the hair spray. It was Katie's diary.

I opened it. '...went down to the river last night with Doug and had some beers. He said he couldn't have many cos of the bike. He's so responsible, not like Stew or Mike. We snogged a bit and he tried to...' I heard someone coming up the stairs so I put it back quickly.

We'd had burgers instead of hot-dogs that night and somebody said something about having burgers at the seaside once that made them ill. Dad joked about going on a holiday together.

'All six of us,' he cheered with a belch, lager can raised high in the air.

'Yeah,' cried Jack, red-faced and shiny, a spattering of ketchup down his shirt.

I counted around the room. Six must mean Katie, too. I was all for that and said so.

They laughed.

I blushed.

Then alcohol made plans for them. There was talk of hiring a caravan, Bournemouth, driving to the New Forest. Great; book it next week. By the end of the conveyor belt they were singing Summer Holiday.

The drive was hot and bad-tempered. Dad couldn't get out of work early so we had to leave late. Mum and Dad had had a row too. Well, not a row exactly, because they didn't have rows; just tense silences. I could tell because when Mum turned the radio on Dad turned it off again with a fast flick of his wrist. Mum refused to look anywhere but out of her passenger window and we didn't stop once all the way down. I was dying for a pee, but didn't dare ask.

When we arrived the others were sitting outside the caravan on deck chairs. Katie had a big floppy hat over her face and her arms trailed over the sides of her deck chair, legs spread wide, feet turned inward. She was wearing a thin, white cotton dress. I could see her bra through it. Much less delicate than I'd imagined it would be. Disappointingly functional. Like two lacy wheelbarrows. She pushed the hat off her face as the usual hello and nice trip? things were said. She smiled at me. I smiled back and tried to walk sexily, like my mum said Paul Newman did. I probably looked as if I'd been in a motorbike accident. Then a youth stepped from the caravan. He was much older than me. Stubbled. Hairy.

Sylvia smiled. 'Oh, everybody...this is Doug. Katie's boyfriend.'

We went into the caravan for a wash and some tea. It was massive inside. I made a joke about the TARDIS. Everybody laughed. I got my hair ruffled and felt stupid in front of Katie and Doug. Science Fiction was kids' stuff; wobbly sets and men in rubber suits.

Sylvia and Jack, it was decided after much good-natured 'No, no, you have it' arguing, would have the proper bedroom, while Mum and Dad would have the pull out sofa-bed in the living room. Katie got the small, triangular second bedroom, and I'd have to sleep on an air-bed on the kitchen floor. With Doug. He gave me a nudge and told me not to try anything. Everybody laughed.

Katie and me were up before everyone else. Doug was still snoring, wrapped in a warm knot of sleeping bag and stale farts, so we decided to go for a little walk.

I thought we looked like a proper couple as we walked toward the site shop. Like the kids I'd seen tied up in tangles of elbows and knees in the park, faces pressed together. She had a purple dress on this time, which was in no way transparent. Mum had left out green shorts and a too-small Spiderman T-shirt for me to wear. I felt stupid; a child. I wanted a leather jacket and jeans, greasy hair, cigarettes, a motorbike. I had the greasy hair, I suppose. And a metallic blue Raleigh Chopper, with speedo.

We stood by the river and I tried to impress Katie with my skimming. There were claims of sixers on the canal back home; but they were from the same guys that said they'd had girls in their rooms. I only ever seemed to be able to manage fours at the most. Stones not flat enough, probably; waves too big. Katie seemed bored. She just stood, looking across the river to the caravans on the other side. A lad with an Alsatian dog was carrying a jerry-can full of water. He had dirty jeans on and a T-shirt wrapped around his waist that dangled around the backs of his knees. Too drunk to funk, it said. You could see the muscles in his arms. He wolf-whistled and waved his free hand. The Alsatian ran around in circles and barked. Katie waved back and smiled.

I skimmed a sixer.

She didn't see.

I sat and watched the ripples die. A duck followed by a trail of grey ducklings left a line in the water that spread out to the bank. A fish left the water, gulped some air, then disappeared again. I looked back at Katie and noticed that she had a faint moustache. Behind her, I saw Doug sauntering along, hands in pockets. He yawned so wide it made his eyes close.

I stood quickly. 'I'm off for some breakfast,' I said. 'Coming?'

They stood together and held hands. 'No thanks,' said Katie, looking at Doug, smiling. 'We'll be along in a bit.'

As I walked away I turned only once, but the long, dry grass on the river bank had already absorbed them.

We went off to the swimming pool at about eleven. Me, Katie, Doug.

I had a bad time. It was full of noisy kids I was scared of because I didn't know them, and women trying to keep their hair dry while being bombed by slippery bodies. I couldn't compete for the diving board or the slide because older lads were using it, performing acrobatics for the groups of girls sitting around the edge in shivering huddles.

Katie and Doug stayed in the deep end, bobbing up and down. There was a sign that said No Petting. They didn't seem to have seen it. Doug's neck rippled as his tongue moved around in Katie's mouth. Below the waterline his body was a blurred clot that occasionally rubbed against Katie's navy blue swimsuit. Every so often she would push him away. He'd get out of the water and do a somersault off the diving board or back dive off the side of the pool. I was bored; ignored. So I waited until they were sitting on the edge, then did a big bomb and soaked them.

The lifeguard blew his whistle at me.

Everybody looked.

When we got out, the changing rooms were full of shouts and the acrobatic older kids flicking wet towels at each other's legs. Doug nodded toward a quiet corner over the other side of the room. 'We'll go over there,' he said. 'Out of the way.'

The cubicles were small and made of dimpled silver metal. They had door catches that wouldn't catch. I slipped off my trunks and they fell into a wet twist on the floor. When I stood up I saw Doug standing outside, naked, wringing his

trunks into a drain. His body was dark with hair. He saw me and looked down at his waist. He smiled.

'Fine specimen, eh?' he said.

I smiled, slightly unsure.

He grinned and stepped close to the door. 'Fancy a closer look?'

I blinked.

Doug glanced up and down the aisle, then pushed into my cubicle. I stepped back. He closed the door behind him and touched my neck with his left hand, rubbing up and around my ear and the back of my neck. His hands were rough, his nails dirty. He pushed my head down and forward.

'No,' I said quietly, twisting away.

He gripped my shoulders, gently turning me around. I was pushed forward, my cheek pressed against the cubicle wall. He held my hips and my feet lifted slightly from the floor. The cubicle shuddered a couple of times. The metal smelled like Dettol. As the kids outside flicked towels and shouted, heat and pain surged through me.

As he let me down, the trunks beneath my right foot squirted cold water.

In the cafe afterwards, Doug bought me a packet of raisin Poppets. Then he spent an hour trying to beat the Galaxian high score. Katie was impressed by his skill, and watched over his left shoulder, smiling.

Their relationship didn't last long after the holiday in Bournemouth. I'd been standing on the stairs one Saturday night soon after, and heard Sylvia say something about Katie being 'better off without him'. Then they'd talked in quiet voices, sharing thoughts plucked from between the lines.

I still see Doug sometimes. He's married with two kids. There's another on the way. If we pass in the street, he says hi, as if we're old mates. His hair's thinner now, and he's got bags under his eyes. Sometimes I'll bump into him in a pub and he'll buy me a drink. We talk briefly about nothing in particular; football, music, television. Once I met Katie at a disco. We hadn't seen each other for a few years and she said how much I'd changed. I thought she'd put on weight. I almost mentioned Doug, just to test the water. But I didn't have the nerve. We just smiled, said see you later, knowing that we probably wouldn't, and went back to the people we'd left swaying in the darkness.

She never mentioned my records. She'd forgotten about them, I suppose. It's scary, the things you can forget.

HITCH

SALENA SALIVA

We picked wild boars and bears,
Ignored the g-naws and tears,
Rips and g-nash in our two hour relationship,
BABY YEAH, I picked you up hitching,

You said 'unusual for a girl to give a guy a ride.'
I said 'unusual to be guilty before tried.'
Now, I had driven listening to your drivel,
FACUOUS, VACUOUS SHALLOW POOLS OF DRIBBLE.

I said 'mind if we stretch our legs, take a walk for a while,'
YOU SAID NOTHING BUT I
OVERHEARD YOU SMILE,
And the sun was surpassing itself in June,
So we took a walk down a forest path for about a mile.

We picked wild flowers for hours, we picked wild flowers,
We picked wild flowers for hours and hours and hours.

I SAID 'MIND IF I SHOOT
YOU IN THE HEAD?'
You laughed until I pumped you with lead,
Got in the van left you to rot,
Pick up another hitcher instead.

For you can rot in the wild flowers for hours,
Or get eaten by boars and bears,
But baby, I promise you won't feel them,
G-NAW RIP, G-NASH AND TEAR,

G-NAW RIP G-NASH AND TEAR,
G-NAW RIP G-NASH AND TEAR.

AUTHOR NOTES

At 17, **Bee** dropped out of school and moved to London from the north of England. A bunch of shady businessmen offered to make him a star, and he became big in Japan fronting a Futurist style Bay City Roller boy band. He then hung up his shoulder pads, went to Thailand for a holiday and never left. He lives in Bangkok where he presents his own Alternative radio show. This story is an extract from novel in progress *Last scene in Siam.*

Steve Bishop lives in Moseley, Birmingham. The author of several short stories published in anthologies and on the internet, he is currently working on a novel.

Bunny has starred in a Manchester band, worked on the successful Teletubbies programme (no details given but our guess is: Tinky Winky?) and is now quitting TV to write full time. All this, and he still looks ludicrously young and sideburned.

Ian Cusack lives in Newcastle upon Tyne where he works as a freelance football writer, dreaming every day of a return 'home' to County Mayo. His fiction has appeared in *Billy Liar* and *Printer's Devil*. He has completed a book of short stories and is currently working on a novel.

Born in London to Polish refugees, **Byrnes** grew up in London and Newcastle. She is currently studying for a PhD at Newcastle University. Her plays have been performed at The Edinburgh Fringe Festival and The Gulbenkian Theatre, Newcastle, and her short stories have appeared in *Billy Liar* magazine.

Daphne Glazer's three short story collections: *The Last Oasis*, *Dressing Up* and *Sex, Love and Loss*, go places her novel, *Three Women*, didn't—tattooists' shops, strip joints, sex shops, hairdressing salons, prisons. Her new novel, *The Cutting Edge*: sex, violence and hairdressing, is published in 1999.

Richard Guest lives in London. He is currently writing a suburban thriller, and completing a book of short stories.

Nik Houghton was raised in Cornwall and now lives and works in the East End of London. He is working on his 153rd novel, a project which will no doubt end in frustration and incompletion. His writing on film and video art has appeared in a range of publications including *New Statesman* and *Artists Newsletter*. He plans to avoid all millennial celebrations.

Anna Landucci is a photographer and a published poet. She *will* be celebrating the millennium, big style.

Toby Litt was born in 1968. He grew up in Ampthill, Bedfordshire. His first two books are a short story collection, *Adventures in Capitalism*, and a novel, *Beatniks*. His new novel, *Corpsing*, will be published by Hamish Hamilton in early 2000.

Revealing dense clouds of angel dust, bubbling moments and an Armalite exitstance, **Morrigan** takes fiction from her own life and gives life to her fiction. She writes in piss and vinegar, devilishly cuntfullble, slurring across the page, blurring a cross reality with the speed of polished thought. Britain's next posthumous genius.

A native Canadian, **Laura Pachkowski** now lives in the West Country. Other published works include a short story in *Fission* (Pulp Faction 1996) and 'The Ghosts of Poland' published in *Women Travel* (Rough Guides 1999).

Salena Saliva is plotting word domination with the release in autumn 1999 of her quarterly concept CDs, *Saltpetre*, and her debut album *Velvet On The Inside*. Salena Saliva exercises regularly and never swears or eat chips.

Sparky is trying not to fall off the edge of the world. Maybe he will succeed.

Martin Sketchley, a freelance writer based in Birmingham, has had work published a range of publications including *The Tiger Garden: A Book of Writers' Dreams*. He is currently working on a science fiction trilogy.

Matt Thorne is the author of *Tourist* and *Eight Minutes Idle.* He is currently co-editing an anthology with Nicholas Blincoe entitled *All Hail the New Puritans* for publication in Autumn 2000.